I HAVE A COMPLAINT TO MAKE!

Fred Carton, at the age of twenty-five, is stranded in a small country town surrounded by bowler hats and umbrellas; he owns neither. He steadfastly refuses to catch an early morning train *anywhere*, let alone to a City office.

If the price of living in this world is working for five days out of seven, he is not sure that the place is worth the price. 'Any fool can go to work,' he says, 'Surviving without it is a much more subtle manoeuvre.'

But Fred's half-hearted attempts to find an alternative fail spectacularly. When he tries to make money, he loses his girlfriend in a poker game . . .

The pressures—and Fred's sense of alienation—increase. Finally he cracks. He buys a gun . . .

An immensely funny book from the author of *THE SECRET LEMONADE DRINKER.*

Also by Guy Bellamy
THE SECRET LEMONADE DRINKER
and published by Corgi Books

I HAVE A COMPLAINT TO MAKE

GUY BELLAMY

CORGI BOOKS

A DIVISION OF TRANSWORLD PUBLISHERS LTD

I HAVE A COMPLAINT TO MAKE

A CORGI BOOK 0 552 11422 7

Originally published in Great Britain by Martin Secker & Warburg Ltd.

PRINTING HISTORY
Secker & Warburg edition published 1979
Corgi edition published 1980

This book is set in Crown.

Corgi Books are published by
Transworld Publishers Ltd.,
Century House, 61-63 Uxbridge Road,
Ealing, London W5 5SA

Printed in the United States by
Offset Paperbacks Inc., Dallas, Pa.

FOR STUART HODGSON:
A friend for twenty-five years

One

I sometimes think that God, in creating
Man, somewhat overestimated His ability.
Oscar Wilde

God is alive and well and working on a
less ambitious project.
Graffito in Bloomsbury

Cardboard Fred decided that there was nothing wrong with him that a miracle wouldn't put right, and after five provocative weeks in the Unit it seemed that only a miracle would help him. God, however, was being His usual inactive self, and that morning Fred arrived finally at the conclusion that assistance, either temporal or spiritual, was by no means on the way. He spent the afternoon in the library, thumbing through Freud and wondering whether he should return to the real world, and then, shortly before tea, Mrs Saunders made the decision for him.

Clearly indifferent to the plum crumble and

custard that was coming up, Mrs Saunders shot herself through the temple with a small German pistol that she had been keeping in her handbag for just such an eventuality. Her death depressed the patients, astonished the nurses and affronted the doctors, who believed that all the quirks in their quirk-ridden establishment had been meticulously documented and understood, and that thieves, alcoholics, deviants and suicides would stick rigidly to what they knew (until they were cured, of course) and not encroach upon one another's territory; for a kleptomaniac to blow the top off her head was not merely tragic, it was perverse.

When the shot reverberated through the long, cream corridors, Fred was reading a book. He knew instinctively that there had been another suicide, but he was surprised that anybody had managed to bring a revolver into the Unit or, indeed, had wanted to. There was nothing that they didn't know about suicide round here, except how to prevent it: sodium amytal tablets' fractional superiority to the razor blade in the hot bath; why gassing was so unpleasant (the limbs getting heavier while the mind raced); the virtues of drowning; the disadvantages of the rubber tube through the car window—they, the patients and the staff, knew it all.

"Who was it?" Fred asked a nurse in the corridor.

The nurse, white-faced, rushed past him shaking her head. Fred followed her but didn't rush. A small crowd, mostly of patients, had gathered outside a second-floor bathroom.

"It's Mrs Saunders," somebody said.

"My God," said a man at the front, pushing through the crowd to get away. Fred caught a glimpse of blood splashed up one wall and decided that he didn't want to see any more, either. He walked slowly along the corridor to his dormitory, took off his jacket and threw it on to a small wooden table which, apart from his bed and a metal locker, was his only furniture.

On the bed lay a fat, blue envelope addressed in

shaky handwriting to him and marked "Private and Confidential". Everything was private and confidential in this place except your eventual death. He lay on the bed, lit a cigarette and thought about Mrs Saunders. She had arrived here only two months ago after a spectacular shop-lifting spree that had nearly brought two businesses to their knees. Given that the place was filled anyway by some extremely unpleasant cases, Mrs Saunders had been one of the few tolerable companions that Fred had found.

He adjusted the pillow and then opened the envelope. A bundle of twenty-pound notes fell on his chest. The letter which accompanied them was from Mrs Saunders, but Fred counted the money twice before he read it. The envelope had contained five hundred pounds.

"Dear Fred, You said the other evening that you thought you would probably find it easier to be happy in this world if you had some money. You said it wasn't something you were sure about but you would like the opportunity to try. I have plenty of money and would like you to accept the enclosed. Please do not mention it to anyone. Henrietta Saunders."

Fred read the letter a second time before returning it to the envelope. Five hundred pounds was so much more than he had ever owned that it was easy for him to imagine lasting indefinitely on it; it was only the rich who enjoyed the luxury of putting money in perspective. He wondered what to do. If Mrs Saunders were still alive he would, through God knows what convention, have gone straight to her room and refused the gift with ill-disguised reluctance. But what could he do now? Without knowing whether her letter preceded her decision to commit suicide, he was left with the possibility that the gift was Mrs Saunders' dying wish, her last will and testament. He could hardly countermand it. And he had another thought: if he kept the money he could get out of this place tomorrow.

He lay on his back, his hands behind his head, and

wondered what he had absorbed from the last five weeks. People seemed to have been talking to him earnestly, incessantly, for most of that time, but how much of it had been of any lasting value to him?

"There is only a narrow distinction," Doctor Jago had told them that morning, "between normal behaviour and neurotic behaviour. Anyone who feels he must touch wood or throw salt over his shoulder, or is plagued by some thought that he cannot get out of his head, or has to return to check whether he has locked his door or shut off the gas, or feels uneasy at the top of a high building or in a dense crowd or an enclosed space, or is ever shy in social situations, or feels inferior or unworthy, is, in a small degree, experiencing the anxieties of a neurotic patient and exhibiting neurotic behaviour."

Fred sat up on the bed. The value of the advice which had been flowing in his direction was questionable. What was not questionable was that now that his wallet was fuller than it had ever been, the need for advice of any sort had receded, if not vanished. He jumped off the bed and headed for Doctor Jago's office.

There were nearly one hundred patients in the Unit, and four doctors. Every morning they split up into small, chatty groups to discuss each other's problems, sometimes helpfully, and three times a week each patient had a private talk with his own doctor. The afternoons were passed gardening in the hospital grounds, or doing woodwork or painting, and in the evenings they played games—cards, badminton, table-tennis, chess—or listened to records. Although they were allowed out, few of them ever went.

At the beginning of every morning they all gathered in the central hall for a talk with the principal, an internationally famous psychiatrist.

"What are we going to do about Eric?" he would ask. "He came in drunk again last night. He knows that drinking will kill him."

The principal liked to involve the whole Unit with problems of this sort, believing that the patients, despite their hurt minds, their excessive sensibilities, their apparent will to fail, were more intelligent, more sensitive than the tougher mortals outside. But he kept bumping his head against the fact that, weak themselves, they were still intolerant of the frailties of others. Many of them seemed to feel that they were in an institution for sane human beings, and behaviour like Eric's merely irritated them.

Fred arrived in the reading-room, where a dozen shabby armchairs were placed round a central table. In one of them sat Enoch the Indecent Assaulter, a gout-ridden technologist whose natural misery had been compounded by the failure of five suicide attempts. But today he was chuckling over a magazine.

"Hallo, Fred," he said. "Did you know that to complain that Schoenberg's **Erwartung** is vitiated by its libretto is to consign oneself to outer darkness? How do they get away with crap like that?"

"Beats me, Enoch. Have you seen Doctor Jago?"

"He's just gone into his office."

"Thanks." Fred paused to look over the magazines that littered the table in the middle of the room. There were no newspapers because nobody wanted to read them. The people in this establishment were not interested in urban terrorism or energy crises, trade deficits or confetti currency; they didn't anguish over the consequences of double-digit inflation. The concerns of other people were not their concerns. Their problem—personal, gigantic and intractable—was how to greet the morning with a smile.

Doctor Jago was happier with women patients and it was hardly surprising. The hospital that he played a large part in running was designed to accommodate a majority of women. One in every nine girls now aged six would get there some day, but only one in every fourteen boys. Women, as Doctor Jago was frequently explaining, had to make so many more adjustments in life, and so far as he was concerned their problems were understandable and their treatment obvious. It was people like Fred, who had not been pregnant or divorced, raped, aborted, deserted or seduced, and who was not, on the copious evidence collected so far, prone to fits of menstrual melancholy, who made the doctor's vocation such heavy going.

Doctor Jago was thirty-nine years old, and his enthusiasm for living was his most formidable weapon in coping with the sad and disconsolate customers who trooped daily into his office. The enthusiasm was as infectious as a cold, and probably lasted just as long, but every now and again somebody who had spent months, even years, cultivating a powerful resentment against society was sent back into it with a smile on his face that he would have found hard to explain.

He was sitting at his desk when Fred walked in, reading the file on one of his patients. Despite his age he was totally bald, which somehow provided an appropriate cupola for his permanent smile.

"Fred. Hallo. Come in," he said.

Fred was never too sure about the smile—smiles could be ambiguous in a way that frowns never were—but he suspected that now that a person had far more chance of being admitted to a mental home than to a university, Doctor Jago was congratulating himself on presiding over a growth industry.

"How are you getting on, Fred? Sit down. How long have you been with us now?"

"Five weeks," said Fred, sitting down. "That's what I wanted to talk to you about. I want to leave."

"To leave?"

"Yes. I'd like to go in the morning."

Doctor Jago placed his hands, palms down, on the desk.

"Well, I don't know about that," he said. "I'll have to study your papers."

Fred looked at the files on Doctor Jago's desk. He didn't want an argument. "I'm not here through a court order. I can discharge myself when I like."

"Oh yes, you can. Certainly." Doctor Jago didn't want to argue, either; in a place like this you never knew where an argument would end. "But naturally we prefer it if patients leave when we say they're ready, not when they say they're ready. Do you feel you're not benefiting?"

"I don't know." Fred crossed his legs. "It's not your fault. But the Unit didn't save Mrs Saunders, did it?"

Doctor Jago leaned forward at his desk, anxious to explain.

"There was no indication of suicidal tendencies, Fred. None whatsoever. But when we know what we're dealing with we have great success. In America and many other countries suicide is now a leading cause of death among young people." He turned up the smile a little. "You vibrant young things with your Messianic dogmas are a problem! However, Britain is one of the few countries where it's not on the increase. We're winning. But a patient must trust his doctor, Fred."

"I try to," said Fred. He didn't feel like a vibrant young thing. "I just don't see where you are getting with me."

Doctor Jago stared at or through his desk. He was writing a book about the relationship between mental and physical illness, but Fred refused to be categorised.

He said: "You arrived here in somewhat strange circumstances. Not many of our patients come direct from a lavatory on Paddington Station."

On the wall behind him, framed in dark wood, was a certificate just as in every cartoon that Fred had ever seen featuring a psychiatrist. He tried to read what it said but the letters were too small.

"Well, what have you learned?" he asked.

It seemed to him that after five weeks of questioning, probing and discussing they should have a clear picture of his problem. He remembered being injected in the first week with a truth drug, but he could only recall their first question: What went wrong with Camilla?

Doctor Jago said: "Depression is like pain. We know it's there but it can sometimes take a little time to find out what's causing it. Your depression is reactive rather than endogenous."

"Is that good?"

"Depression is never good, Fred, and always complicated. I could talk to you about the hypothalamic-pituitary-adrenal control mechanism."

"I'd rather you didn't." Doctor Jago could be a shade prolix if you let him.

"The adrenal gland is sometimes a crucial factor," he said, "but five weeks is no time at all to get to the bottom of these things. How old are you, Fred?"

"Twenty-five."

Doctor Jago nodded. "Well, of course you can go if you want to. This isn't a prison." He drummed his fingers on the desk. "Look, come and see me tomorrow. I'll have a look at your papers. If you want to leave, you can, but I'd like you to sleep on it."

Fred stood up.

"Thanks," he said.

"How's the chess going?"

"I think I'm the Unit champion. It's a bit difficult to tell. Mr McGivern kicks the table over when he loses his queen."

"Mr McGivern," said Doctor Jago. "I don't know what's the matter with him."

What I would like, thought Cardboard Fred the following afternoon as he arrived in the place that for want of a better name he called home, is for a monumental and extremely smelly pudding to be dropped on this town from an immense height. He imagined the event in some detail and then selected half a dozen people, living on the town's outskirts, who could usefully be felled by a few stray globules, detached in descent from the main body.

He walked down the station steps, his belongings in one not very large hold-all, and, seeing the trees and the ornate old buildings, wondered whether he wasn't already missing the excitement of London; of course, when he was in London he craved for the tranquillity of the country.

It was an old town that had depended on cloth-making in the seventeenth century, corn in the eighteenth, hops in the nineteenth and the 7.45 a.m. train to London in the twentieth. Its proudest possessions were a twelfth-century manor house which was mentioned in **Green's Guide to the Home Counties**, and a Benedictine abbey built a mere six hundred years ago. The buildings now were mostly Georgian and the inhabitants were mainly Victorian, battling vainly against every new development, physical, social or political, and nimbly dropping one fight to launch another as progress hit them from all directions; when capital punishment was abolished they had seven thousand signatures on a petition demanding the return of the cat.

Fred walked across the station yard in the sunshine and into the town. His programme was vague and his hopes were as low as usual; only his wallet, bulging unnaturally with the excitement of twenty-five twenty-pound notes, gave him a different feeling in the pit of his stomach.

It was a town without men. They were away during the daylight hours, fighting the good fight in a thousand air-conditioned offices so that their wives could pick up the children from school in large, noiseless limousines. It was a way of life that had no appeal to Fred. While the workers hurried, lemming-like, towards their first coronary, he survived in idle poverty—better to live on your knees than die on your feet. Mysteriously, it was also a town of spinsters, their pale faces reflecting a lifetime of self-imposed deprivation—not only deprivation of fun, extravagance or sex, but a wholesale eschewing of anything likely to promote the semblance of a smile. They hurried among the shoppers, nervously protecting a virginity that was no longer threatened, if it ever had been.

Fred had a flat over a small pet shop on the edge of the town. He had taken it on a five-year lease three years ago and the rent, which was low then, now, with inflation, seemed nominal. He had a bedroom, a bathroom, a living-room and a kitchen, all on the same floor.

He had lived here alone for two years, but in the last twelve months he had acquired the company of a particularly resourceful mouse. His first and last attempt to eject the unpaying guest, perhaps a refugee from the pet shop downstairs, had been planned with military precision. Fred borrowed a modern super-trap, chose the cheese with loving care and prepared an ambush that should have stunned a dog. When he went in the following morning to formally cremate the body, the trap was upside down, the cheese was gone, and there was mouse turd all over the floor. He had half-expected to find a note from the mouse.

Climbing the wooden steps at the side of the pet shop which led up to his flat's door, he wondered what mountain of mail would be waiting for him on the mat. But when he had let himself in he found that the world had sent him very few messages. A note from Trader Ryan saying, "Come out, come out, wherever you are," was at the top of the pile, lying across an electricity bill. Then came an invitation to subscribe to a new monthly magazine which promised to tell you all you needed to know about car engines but were too bored to ask, and beneath it was a seed catalogue for the previous occupant-but-three who died nine years ago and had herself probably manured some of the lurid growths illustrated for her appraisal. At the bottom of the heap was a two-week-old letter from his mother in Dover, which he opened immediately to make sure that nothing too disastrous had happened on the family front. Nothing at all had happened on the family front.

He carried the lot—five weeks' mail—into his bedroom and unpacked. A huge, under-used double bed was at the centre of the room. Three of the pale blue walls bore a map: one of Britain, a second of Europe, a third of the world, all of which Fred had studied, sometimes for hours. There were, he had discovered, strangely therapeutic benefits to be derived from knowing where Dahomey was, or Burundi or the Bering Strait: it somehow helped to diminish his problems. When he had hung up his shirts in the battered wardrobe that stood at the side of his bed, and returned socks and pants to the drawers allotted to them, he wandered through to the tiny kitchen to see what food had been left after his sudden departure five weeks before. The flat was so poorly furnished that it had the cheerless air of very temporary accommodation rather than of a home; the kitchen seemed to be the only room that was half-way equipped. On the electric cooker was a chip pan, a frying pan and a kettle; on the floor nearby was an orange plastic pedal bin whose matching bowl stood on its side in the steel sink. He opened the room's solitary cupboard, high up on the wall next to the Ascot gas heater. Saucepans, plates and canned food filled the shelves, along with some old beer mugs and packets of soup mix. He found a tin of sausages and some beans, reached for the tin-opener and turned on the cooker.

Thus was Cardboard Fred returned to the real world.

In the centre of the town, at the junction of its two main streets, a sixteenth-century coaching inn had become an ivy-covered, three-star hotel. Inside, timber-framed walls bore tarnished souvenirs of a presumably romantic past: coachmen's whips, maps, brasses, post horns. Christopher Marlowe drank there once; Cardboard Fred drank there many times in a very special bar below the surface of the earth.

From the cobbled street you went down a dozen steps to the Cellar Bar and sat at an oak counter on stools that were made from old beer barrels, and covered in padded leather. It was here that the people who were making money in this town sipped expensive liquor, talked loudly, beamed affably, before hurrying off to rob their employees, cheat their customers and bilk the taxman. But today there was a treat. Sitting at the bar as Fred came down the steps was Dermot Ryan.

If a man's life is written on his face, things had not gone too well for Dermot Ryan. Becoming a local legend had taken its toll, and at thirty-six he looked about fifty. He was a bulky, untidy-looking man who ran a junk shop in the town, but still managed to devote more time and energy to pleasure than even the most nervous worker did to his job. His battered beer-drinker's face creased into a grin when he saw Fred approach.

"Cardboard Fred," he said, stumbling across the bar. "I thought you'd defected. Here, let me give you my card." From the top pocket of his khaki army shirt he pulled a handful of personal cards which said: "Trader Ryan—Antique Dealer."

"Trader Ryan, antique dealer, washing taken in and superfluous hair painlessly removed," said Fred, pretending to read the card. "Let me buy you a drink."

"That is an idea whose time has come, Frederick. Where in hell have you been?"

Fred smiled broadly: it seemed a long time since he had. "I've been around and about," he said. "What are you drinking this week?"

"You've been away for at least a month. I've called at your flat and hurled abuse through the letter-box. No one answered. I'll have a lager."

"Well, I'm back now. Don't you think I look well?"

Cardboard Fred at twenty-five was a little over six feet tall and two stone lighter than the recommended weight for someone of his height. His round face was pale, even in the summer, and his large blue eyes revealed rather too easily what he was feeling.

Dermot studied him. "Let me put it this way," he said. "What do you charge to haunt a house?"

Fred bought two pints of lager from a tall, dark-haired barmaid who had appeared on the pay-roll in his absence. It was a welcome appointment: in the past the hotel had seemed to recruit its staff from the geriatric ward.

"Name's Miranda," said Dermot. "She can sit on my face any time."

"She seems to have all the requisite bits and pieces," said Fred, admiring her shape.

"You don't get many of those to the pound. Cheers."

He took his pint and Fred looked around the small, oblong bar. It was too early for there to be too many customers in yet, just a few of the respectable marrieds who drank one pint before going home. They would be replaced later by the less respectable unmarrieds, who went home first and then drank ten pints.

Dermot lifted one thigh over a stool at the bar.

"Where's the beautiful Camilla?" he asked.

Fred wondered, too. "Search me," he said.

"Is it over? Then you must find a new lady. I keep telling you. Life's too short for celibacy."

"Don't worry about me," said Fred, putting his drink on the bar. "I'm quite used to curling up in bed on my own every night."

Dermot chuckled. "The soixante without the neuf," he murmured. "Listen, you shouldn't have any trouble in replacing her. You're the answer to a maiden's prayer."

"I quite agree," said Fred. "But when did you last see a praying maiden? It's easy for you married men."

Dermot drank some lager and looked rueful. "Easy? It's not easy. It's not even fun half the time. Do you know what I really want? I was thinking about it the other day. Do you know the one thing I'd really love to have?"

Fred shook his head solemnly.

"What do you really want, Trader?"

Dermot leaned forward, confidentially. "What I'd really like is an uncommitted erection. All mine are spoken for. I want one I can please myself with." He looked genuinely sad. "My old lady's thirty next month. I'm thinking of trading her in for a couple of fifteen-year-olds."

"I shouldn't think you'd get many uncommitted erections if you do that."

Trader Ryan shrugged. "You can't have everything."

But it seemed to Fred that within the limited options that were open to anybody, Trader did have everything. His marriage, to a wife whom Fred had scarcely seen, imposed no restraints on his wild and eccentric existence. He worked when he wanted to, drank when he wanted to, disappeared for days on end when he felt like it, indulged every fancy and gratified every whim. He had over the years arrived in the Cellar dressed as a cowboy, a High Court judge, a Crimean soldier and a priest, and nobody took any notice. One day when he bounded in as a frighteningly realistic gorilla, people just said, "Evening, Trader," and carried on drinking. He once went into a public house on Christmas Eve with £146 in his pocket and emerged on New Year's Day without a penny. But his marriage survived, perhaps because he could make money very quickly when he had to. His motto at the junk shop was

"SPQR", which he explained meant small profits, quick returns. But sometimes he added with an evil grin that it also stood for silly people quickly robbed.

He finished his lager and beckoned Miranda. She came up to him smiling and he pushed his empty glass towards her.

"What about an assignation in the park tonight?" he asked. "I'll make it worth your while. Okay?"

"Don't beg, Trader. It doesn't suit you. Lager?"

"I'm not begging. I'm grovelling." He turned to Fred as she took the glass away. "She shaves herself, you know."

"I didn't. How did you?"

"A friend took her out. Can't stand women who shave themselves. Picking pubic hairs out of your teeth is one of the few pleasures left in this world. Lager, Fred?"

"Thanks."

Fred got himself one of the beer-barrel stools and sat at the bar. It was good to be home, but how long could it last? Train fares and lager had already reduced his £500 to £497. Merely staying alive eroded your assets: breathing cost money. He sipped his new pint of lager and tried to fix the area of thought that his mind would be allowed to meander through. There would be no thinking about Camilla. There would be no thinking about work.

"How long could a man last around here on five hundred pounds?" he asked.

"You've got five hundred pounds? I **thought** you'd been away earning money. Well, I maximise the bartering system, myself. I give them a table, they mend my car."

A woman sitting with her friend in the wall seats was announcing proudly that her aspidistra had had triplets. A pale young man with a sparse blond beard had just come in with a girl who revealed that she and her parents failed to communicate by a million light years.

"I mean survive without working," said Fred.

"I'm not cut out to be a wage-slave."

"Nor am I. That's why I work for myself."

Fred shook his head glumly. "The people round here lead a conveyor-belt existence that frightens me to death. Getting up, going to the office, coming home, watching television, going to bed. I don't want that. But what else is there?"

Dermot pulled a half-smoked cigar from his shirt pocket.

"You've come home in a very lugubrious frame of mind," he said. "Work in a bar. You spend most of your life in them already."

"I worked in a bar once," said Fred. "It nearly put me off drinking. What I want is to know that when I'm old I've made some worthwhile use of my life. That's what. We're here for a purpose, and dirging around selling beer isn't it. Think of all the people in this execrable town. What **can** they say to themselves when they're dying? What **awful** regrets they must have."

Dermot replied slowly. "I'll tell you why we're here. We're here to till the soil, to create beautiful things, to reproduce ourselves." He looked at Fred, rather pleased with his analysis. "You're doing none of those things, which is why your mentality is such a terrible shambles."

"I'm creating a rather beautiful poem at the moment, as a matter of fact. It's called 'Coffins Are Comfortable'."

"Very good," said Dermot. "All you need now is a plot of land and a beautiful lady and your personality will blossom. You had a beautiful lady once—you should never have lost a girl like that. They don't grow on trees. If they did we'd all work for the Forestry Commission. I know about these things, kiddo. I didn't come down with last night's rain."

It was rain that had become permanently entangled with his picture of her—violent rain, torrential rain, rain that bounced a yard off the street. On the first, memorable night that they met, only a few months earlier, it had been coming down like stair-rods. Oddly, it had turned out to be the only rain of the summer.

She was a short girl, five feet three or four, with long, blonde hair that hung down to her waist, a conventionally pretty face but with big eyes and big, full lips that seemed more suited to some activities than others. The green eyes were an invitation and the mouth was a promise. In the first few moments he had gazed at her incredulously—after so many years, here she was.

That night she was wearing a tight, black sweater and blue jeans that seemed to have been melted on to her bottom. Round her neck and outside the sweater hung a silver chain, and from the chain hung a tiny silver Coca-Cola bottle.

It was after midnight in a smoky, crowded discotheque where the ravings of the house disc-jockey and the decibels at his disposal made verbal contact difficult, full conversation impossible.

Fred had been persuaded to drop in on this teenage carnival by Dermot, who was running one of his periodic campaigns to get Fred engaged, married, tied down. Fred had a theory that married men had a grudge against single men, but he was quite keen to find a girl himself.

"I don't think a discotheque is going to produce the goods," he had said. "All the girls are about fourteen."

"What's wrong with that?" Dermot replied. "Fourteen your unlucky number?"

Fred went along on his own, and now he stared in astonishment. He and Dermot had between them raked the ashes of the district's sexual possibilities: they had never even seen this exotic creature. The explanation came later. Camilla's father was in the Air Force and he had been posted to the area only the previous day. A week earlier, Camilla had been sunning herself in Singapore.

Having spent years avoiding rebuffs, Fred had learned finally and for good that more than half of the young ladies around would never rebuff anybody but were constantly, secretly praying to be asked. He moved quickly through the crowd that was twitching on the central dance-floor: young people didn't dance any more, they stood around and shook.

Soon he was beside her, surprised at her smallness. He smiled at her; she looked up at him. After four pints of beer there was little chance of his asking whether she came here often.

"I've been searching for you for years," he said.

She looked at him for three or four seconds, but her expression gave nothing away.

"That's the most beautiful mouth I've ever seen," he told her. "Have you had it long?"

Finally she smiled. "If you want to sleep with me tonight you can," she said. "You don't have to wade through that stuff."

For reasons that were far from obvious, Fred was very much in favour of taking her to bed as soon as possible. All his happiest relationships with women had started with immediate sex; it provided the correct basis for their friendship from the beginning. Other girls, who had successfully retained his affection while at the same time delaying their debut in the bedroom, had found when they finally arrived there, after weeks or even months, that he had difficulty in viewing them sexually. They had become a pal of indeterminate gender and sex was often beyond his powers, sometimes for days.

He took her hand and led her to the quietest corner of the club where youngsters drank coffee and soft drinks. In a short time he knew a lot about her.

"Why did you say that I could sleep with you tonight when you didn't even know me?" he managed to ask after half an hour.

"Well," she said, laughing, "it's true."

Outside in the rain they dodged from doorway to doorway.

Camilla held his hand firmly and asked: "What do

you do, Fred? You're not a sword-swallower, are you? I've always wanted to go out with a sword-swallower." She had a voice that sounded as if it had received professional training, a training that had not quite eradicated a giggle—almost a gurgle—that lay at the back of it.

Fred listed a few jobs that he had held over the past few years so that she wouldn't think him lazy, but stopped short after six in case she thought him feckless.

"My head's in a whirl," she shouted. "You're imparting too much information in one go!"

By the time they reached Fred's flat the downpour had soaked them but they fell on each other hungrily, not noticing. He took her jeans off first and she lay on her back on the floor, as he pulled them up over her feet. Naked, she was unselfconscious.

"What do you want me to do?" she asked, briskly. "I'll do anything you want, and afterwards I'll tell you what I want you to do."

Fred was intrigued. The girls in his past had never been so explicit. He shed his clothes with an expert's speed and joined her on the bed. She had been sun-bathing topless and her breasts, which were large even when she was lying on her back, were as brown as the rest of her body. Below her waist the tiny white triangle that the sun had never seen barely covered her pubic hair.

"Well?" she said.

"If we could tie one ankle to the light cord and the other to the top of the door, you could sort of swing . . ."

"Don't be ridiculous, Fred."

"Do you want the light out?"

"No, I want to look at you."

He kissed her breasts and ran his hand up her leg.

"What do you want me to do?" he asked. "Challenge me."

She lay back on the dark green duvet, her legs fractionally apart.

"What I'd like," she said, "I mean, it's up to you. I

don't want you to do it if you don't fancy it. It's up to you."

There was something a little nutty about this girl, a flaw that was difficult to locate.

"Come on," he said.

"Lick me."

He slid willingly down the bed, running his tongue over her flat, hard stomach. He could almost taste the sun. He buried his face between her legs: there was a warm, neutral smell, like coal. He pushed, licked, kissed. Camilla squirmed. After a while she pulled him up and demanded that they make love conventionally, slowly, thoughtfully.

"I'm not going to fake anything," she said.

Fred smiled to himself at her attitude. The women's lib movement might not have made much progress elsewhere, but it had taken over the bedroom.

"Nor am I," he said.

Camilla laughed and pushed her body towards him.

When they had finished, she said: "More! More!" He didn't know whether he had failed to satisfy her, or whether her appetite was just unusually large. He lay on his side to study this strange girl who he had known for only an hour and who a few days earlier had been half a world away. He wondered whether he was, at last, in love. The trouble with saying "I love you" was that you had to go on saying it. Once you had said "I love you", nothing less would do.

Camilla rolled away from him and found a Kleenex in her bag. She stuffed it between her legs.

"What nobody ever told me about sex was how **messy** it is," she said. "All those books and films and you never saw a woman reaching for a Kleenex. It's so **messy**!"

She screwed up her face and Fred kissed it.

The following evening they walked for two miles out into the pine and heather country, and lay on the sand by a lake used by a sailing club at weekends.

Above them, silver birch trees lined the pond, and on either side purple heather stretched away across the common. The road and the traffic were half a mile away and the car horn noises of the coots in the reeds was the only sound to reach them.

"What are you going to do, pudding?" Camilla asked. She was wearing a white blouse that emphasised her suntan, and red jeans.

"I don't know."

"It seems so strange for someone of your age not to have a career. You're not expecting a legacy, are you?"

"I'm afraid not."

"Is there nothing you want to do?"

"No."

"That's terrible."

He waved a hand. "My life is an unbroken series of unsuccessful gestures," he said. "I've had dozens of jobs and I've hated all of them. I wouldn't mind being Prime Minister, but where do you start? I write poems, but they aren't very good. I'd like to be a professional sportsman or a film director or an airline pilot or one of those poker-faced young men who are rude to politicians on television. But I could never endure the years of rubbish that you have to put up with before you get a nice job like that."

Camilla sighed. "What I'd really like to do is photograph elephants in Africa," she said. "I'll get a camera, and you can write poems to go with the pictures. We'll show 'em!"

Fred grinned at her **naïveté.** "You never show 'em," he told her. "You never show anybody. You just remove the need to."

He watched the coots rowing through the water. The feeling that he was different in some quite seriously disadvantageous way was nudging at the edges of his mind.

"Why do they call you Cardboard Fred, anyway?" Camilla asked.

"Because my surname is Carton. Cardboard

Carton. It's a joke by a friend of mine called Dermot Ryan."

"I thought it was something else."

"What?"

"Cardboard crumples. It folds up under pressure."

It was a shrewd stab that he was to remember later.

He raised himself on an elbow and looked down at her. To his surprise she had undone her blouse and was wearing no bra. Her breasts were displayed for every Peeping Tom.

"I have an idea that I am falling in love with you," he said, reaching for them.

"Only an idea?"

"Only an idea, but it's beginning to gel, it's beginning to coalesce. It's beginning to adhere to the sides."

He was attracted by her guilelessness and, more than that, by her enthusiasm and directness. Not for her the "what a bore" expression with which so many young girls attempted to disguise their inadequacies. And she was sexy, too—genuinely sexy. Most girls didn't bare their breasts unasked. For some reason, even in the sexually exhausting weeks that followed, the simple truth that she was a nymphomaniac didn't occur to him.

In the cinema the following evening, while Fred struggled to follow the heart-tugging portait of a young postulant's spiritual dilemma, she unzipped his jeans and disappeared into his lap, sucking soundlessly until the national anthem disturbed them both. On a riverboat shuffle on the Thames they locked themselves into a lavatory as the boat slid beneath the lights of Hampton Court Bridge, and emerged, only temporarily sated, at Molesey Lock. Sitting opposite each other at dinner in the poshest restaurant in the town he took off his right sandal and gave her an orgasm under the table with his big toe. At Climping, on the south coast, they sun-bathed naked in the sand dunes of a deserted beach and then made love in the water because Camilla said that elephants did. They coupled at every opportunity that came along and sometimes when none did. Once they managed it horizontally on the top deck of a bus while the conductor loitered curiously below, and afterwards did it vertically in the bus shelter when they alighted. The possibility of discovery gave an edge to their lovemaking that was missing in a bedroom. Not that they needed the additional stimulus. There were no boundaries to their lust and seemingly no means of exhausting it; it was elastic, it was eternal, it was bottomless.

Eventually Camilla's parents, who had invested heavily in their only daughter's education, suggested that she find a good job, but she didn't have the time. She began to look as if she had seen the Second Coming and her dizziness perplexed them.

Occasionally she perplexed Fred.

Once she said: "You should get yourself a decent woman," and mystified him. But he was gone, hooked, fazed and sold; a lifetime of disappointments seemed a small price to pay for knowing how lucky he was now.

It lasted for one wild month. By that time, already two weeks late, Camilla knew that she was pregnant.

Two

Is there a life after birth?
American button slogan

On Saturday mornings the town, by some mysterious alchemy, assumed a different character. It was almost as if the set had been changed by a theatrical hand, and the lighting altered. The people who ambled round its sunny streets had escaped after five days' confinement, a recurring sentence of penal servitude, and remission for good behaviour gave them Saturdays. They celebrated their parole by wearing different expressions and different clothes. It was the brightest hour of the week, as Sunday was the bleakest. On Sunday there was nothing to hope for.

Fred rose early on his first day home. Working or not, Saturday was always special to him, too. He put on jeans and an old tartan shirt and found a silver chain bracelet that Camilla had given him. He then spent a pleasant ten minutes counting his money. He had £493 left. It was a sum that many people would have found derisory, but it was more than he had ever had in the flat and it pushed the necessity for work into the hazy distance.

He left the flat soon after ten and wandered into town at a distinctly Saturday morning pace, looking at girls, watching for old friends. There were always more people around at weekends. At the end of the town, where dentists, chiropodists, chartered accountants and solicitors did business in converted Georgian houses, he reached the newsagents and went in to buy some cigarettes. There was a contents bill for the local paper propped up outside which said: "Local Man's Alarming Mishap." A perspicacious bull terrier was nonchalantly but accurately urinating over it. Outside, a man was walking along the gutter carrying a board which said: "He Who Hath The Son Hath Life." Whatever his message, this was altogether too complicated a way of putting it, and people hurried by embarrassed as if his notice had said: "My Trousers Are Undone."

Fred walked slowly back to the centre of the town where the supermarkets and chemists and television rental firms paid the rates. Tucked between them was a coffee bar. Fred took a table that commanded a view of the crowded street, but once he had sat down he read the paper that he had bought with his cigarettes. A girl bank clerk had been shot dead during a £20,000 raid in London; a Bulgarian airliner had been hi-jacked; a seventy-four-year-old millionaire, the head of a chain of underwear stores, had been kidnapped in Austria. Everywhere people were trying to make money.

Fred remembered when he had struggled over money. He remembered when a five-pound note solved all problems, and now he had almost a hundred of them. He could remember his first pocket money and the plane kit that he bought with it.

His childhood had recently become vivid again, because he had done a lot of remembering lately:

that was what the Unit wanted you to do. Five weeks in the Unit was a trip down Memory Lane, back-tracking over your life, investing trivial, half-forgotten incidents with portentous psychological significance.

He had remembered hanging grass-hoppers.

Two men had been hanged in London and another was going to be hanged soon as well. The non-stop activities of the hangman obsessed his young mind, and so he and his friends invented a game: hang a grass-hopper. The noose of string was tied to the clothes-line. Grass-hoppers were caught, charged, condemned, dispatched. It didn't seem to mean a lot to the grass-hoppers, but twenty years on those grisly ceremonies on the lawn still haunted him.

They made him remember beatings-up at school.

The classroom was a wooden shack where the ink froze solid in the winter so that they had to write with pencils. The teachers were mostly priests—sadists, masochists, pederasts. Sharing their apparently meagre knowledge with thirty frightened school-boys was a respectable front for more nefarious activities. Some left suddenly after being discovered with their hands in sleeping boys' beds; others survived indefinitely on the edge of disgrace. Many obtained sexual gratification from wild displays of violence. He remembered the bloodstained arrival of Father Reilly, a short, stocky French-teacher who specialised in the pre-emptive strike. He burst into the classroom on his first morning, plunged between the desks and hauled a boy to his feet by his hair so that he could punch him in the face. Five times the boy hit the floor, his face covered with blood, and five times Father Reilly pulled him up again ignoring his screams for mercy. "Don't hit me again, Father," the boy shrieked. He was eight. Father Reilly, red-faced and aroused, continued throwing punches from awkward angles. Fred went home that day with flecks of blood on his shirt and vowed that when he was older he would intercept Father Reilly in the street and rearrange his face. He looked forward to how the public would receive the news: THUG BEATS UP PRIEST.

The Unit had also been very enthusiastic about persuading him to remember Camilla, but he was saved from re-treading that sad path by the sight of Trader Ryan through the coffee bar window. He was carrying a small black puppy and heading for the Cellar. Fred paid and left.

The Cellar on Saturday lunchtime attracted an entirely different bunch of customers from those who used the place at other times of the week. This was because a large number of the town's younger generation worked in London, and rather than travel up daily they lived eight to a flat during the week in Canonbury or Kensington, Islington or Chelsea. At weekends they came home to see their families. They called it "going to the country" and armed with a spurious metropolitan sophistication they spent a lot of the weekend complaining about what a hick town this was.

At the centre of this social phenomenon, Trader Ryan was trying to sell the puppy.

"It seems such a damned shame," he said. "He's such a friendly little thing."

"What's a shame?" said a toothy young girl.

"I only want five pounds for him. Only five pounds. He's half Labrador, you know." He ran a finger gently up the puppy's nose. It looked up at Dermot and blinked.

"What's a shame?" the girl asked again.

"Oh, he'll have to be put down this afternoon. I can't keep him."

"You can't do that," said another girl. "He's a lovely animal."

Dermot surveyed the gathering audience. Nobody wanted to buy the puppy.

"Can't afford a vet," he said dismally. "I'll have to give it the hammer."

"I'll buy it," said the toothy girl. A five-pound note

appeared rapidly from her handbag. Dermot gave her the puppy and came over to Fred.

"Never fails," he said. "That's the third one I've sold this week. Pint of Holsten?"

"At least."

They managed, despite the weekend influx, to get their usual stools at the bar.

"I've been thinking about what you said last night," said Dermot, lighting his cigar. "About you and Camilla. Why exactly has it ended? What happened?"

"A gentleman doesn't kiss and tell."

"You a gentleman?"

"I'm working at it."

"What I want to know is what happened to the torrid jungle passion of April?"

"It's become the icy tundra wastes of July."

"Where is she? Why ain't she here, proffering her parts?"

"I give in. Why ain't she?"

"Bloody hell," said Dermot, gazing behind Fred's shoulder. "Oliver Oswald, your friendly neighbourhood bigot, has just come in. Disguise yourself as a tree or something."

Fred saw Oliver Oswald approaching through the crowd. "Buy your councillor a drink," he said. "You never know when he might come in useful."

Dermot shook his head. "Buying that man a drink is like covering yourself in horseshit when there are flies around. Just when you were going to tell me what happened to Camilla!"

The humbling truth was that he didn't know what had happened to her, and now he hardly dared to think about it. Lifted more than he could have imagined by the news that they were to have a baby, he was destroyed immediately by the discovery that her reaction was quite different.

"Let's get married," he said when she arrived at his flat to break the news. It was not only what he thought she wanted him to say, it was what he wanted to say, too. He could see the infant in a pram in the hall already, the magic ingredient that his life had lacked, purpose.

"Marry?" said Camilla, doubtfully.

He thought that she meant that the word was out of fashion and he hastened to correct himself.

"Well, move in with me anyway. Marry when you want to. I was just thinking of your parents. I love you. Did I mention it?"

"I'm too young to marry," said Camilla. "I'm too young to have a baby, as well."

She sat in an armchair in his living-room and stared into her own lap. "I've only just got back to England after three years away. I'm nineteen years old, pudding. I'm looking forward to fun, fun, fun. Nappies and washing-machines can come later."

Fred didn't say anything. He could see tricycles and train sets, sand-pits and paddling pools. It was just what he needed.

Presently she stood up.

"Come and buy me some gin."

"You don't drink gin."

"It might bring my period on."

The gin didn't work. She had several uncomfortable hot baths. They didn't work and he bought her some tablets from a chemist he knew and they didn't work either.

On a blue May day, when the first real heat of the summer was settling, they went to the coast and Camilla swam with a frantic energy.

Afterwards they lay on the beach.

"It's no use, pudding."

"Good," said Fred, taking her hand. "Let's get married."

"It will have to be an abortion."

Fred let go of her hand.

"Don't be silly," he said.

"What's silly about it?"

"Well," he said weakly, "abortions cost money."

"If you can't afford an abortion you can't afford a marriage."

Fred sensed that some residual influences from what he took to be a privileged upbringing were now surfacing to reject him: as a husband-to-be he was a non-starter. No job, no money, no ambition, no hope. He tried another approach.

"It's a life," he said. "At least, the Catholics say it is."

"If the Catholics really believe it's a life, why don't they have a funeral service when a woman has a miscarriage? Of course it's not a life. It's a slightly irregular physical condition that has to be corrected."

Fred lay on his back and looked up at a cloud that was threatening to come between him and the sun.

"Your steel is showing, Camilla. What happened to the beautiful little girl?"

"Needs must," said Camilla. "I have a girlfriend in London who can probably help. I'm not going to a doctor and paying a fortune, and I'd never get it on the National Health."

Camilla arranged it all quite easily, and a fortnight later the two of them caught an evening train to London.

It was an almost empty train: at this time of day all the human traffic was going the other way. They sat opposite each other, surprisingly awkward. Camilla looked out of the window, avoiding his eyes.

Once he said: "Change your mind?" but she only shook her head.

He stared out of the window at row after row of new box houses, all concealing, no doubt, new wife and new car. How did so many young men accumulate so much so quickly? Did they marry their pregnant girlfriends and discover that necessity is indeed the mother of invention? He lit a cigarette, saw that he was in a non-smoker and stubbed it out. For the rest of the journey they read in silence the magazines that each had bought at the station. Fred read an article headed "Energy versus Ecology: Is this a realistic confrontation?" Camilla read "The Do's and Don'ts of dating".

Camilla's friend met them at Paddington. She was a tall, brisk public school girl who embraced Camilla and glowered at Fred as if it had just been proved, beyond doubt and much to everyone's surprise, that he was personally responsible for most of the world's misery.

"Who has the money?" she asked, looking at him.

Fred handed her a hundred pounds. It came out of what he had saved during a winter job in a factory, mostly through overtime, and giving it to the girl left him with less than fifty.

"We'll be about an hour," the girl told him. "Where will you wait?"

"In the bar?" Fred suggested.

Horrified, he watched them walk away, overwhelmed by a feeling of helplessness. The reality of what was going to happen bit into him now; he had always been very good at not looking anything in the face until he could practically smell its breath. He headed for the bar, found a stool at the counter, and ordered the first large whisky of his life.

The whisky provided a calm veneer which cloaked his total disintegration.

He called the barmaid and ordered another and another.

Some people think that drinking alcohol is the most fatuous waste of time since the invention of the piano lesson, but this isn't so, he announced to himself.

The barmaid had dewlaps.

"Forty pence," she said.

A spot of moisture hit his cheek. Could she possibly be spitting from that distance? Perhaps she was some sort of champion. He handed her the money and drank the whisky.

Don't go away, dewlapped lady. I have another green whisky voucher here somewhere. He pulled a pound note from his pocket as the barmaid returned. His head was ringing already.

A woman with a beard came in. Something wrong there. Either it wasn't a woman or it wasn't a beard. It wasn't a woman. It's so confusing these days, Inspector.

He put his hands to his temples and closed his eyes.

Dear Sir or Madman, I am sitting here not waiting for the 7.28 to wifey, nor am I about to go out on the town in this sick, stinking metropolis of ours. No. Negative. My presence here tonight is in the role of a fairly exalted extra in one of life's rich human dramas (act one, scene far too many). Make with the Scotch, Miss World. Still only forty pence? You're practically giving it away.

Somewhere out there in a taxi, heading, I believe, in the Clapham direction, is easily the most beautiful girl I have ever met, beautiful and sexy.

The taxi will drop her and her friend near the underground station, I understand, and there they will wait until a green Jaguar—or a blue Hillman or a black Ford—pulls up at the kerb. Only one passenger will climb into the car, a hundred pounds will change hands, and they will drive off by a circuitous route to a house in one of the world's backstreets.

How will Camilla be feeling by this time? Better not kick that idea around too much. Better leave that one alone. Seems to be some mistake. Glass dry on inside as well as outside. Finger out, Miss Dewlaps. Takes ten years to get served in here. Man Dies Of Thirst In London Bar: Woman Held.

Where was I? The driver of the car will be a flashy young man, taking furtive looks at the lovely Camilla through the rearview mirror. In the front passenger seat will be a woman in her late thirties, a retired midwife—retired on account of midwives can't make three hundred tax-free oncers in a week. The car radio will be on loud, with a speaker behind the back seat. It will be a journey of less than ten minutes.

All things considered, by and large, weighing one thing against another, I feel hideous. Prognosis: poor. The forecast for tonight: a cold front is moving in from the Azores with a hostile expression on its face. Presently, shortly, and by and by, I am going to be not at all well. It's that old heavy feeling under the tongue. Press your jaw, that used to fix it. Well, it ain't gonna fix it tonight.

Barmaid, there you are. You get harder to find as the night wears on. Scotch, please. Oh, you knew. Marvellous. Shall I compare thee to a summer's day? No, I don't think I will. You look awful disapproving. Beware, madam. I have a reputation among the cognoscenti of the genre for the one-liner that wounds.

Where did I leave you, Camilla? **Why** did I leave you, Camilla?

The good woman, the former midwife, will lead you along a corridor into a room at the back of the house. She will leave you sitting there, and go through to a kitchen to put a kettle on. Then she will call to ask whether you have brought any towels and you will discover how nervous you are when you try to call that you haven't.

Camilla sitting there, waiting, wondering, scared now, and the kettle warming up outside.

Nobody ain't gonna believe this, but mah lil ole glass is plumb empty agin. Move over, tumbleguts. Fred's turn for the firewater. This here bar is as gay and as lively as the cold, cobbled streets of Edinburgh on New Year's Day. Feeling lonely? Fart—someone's bound to stand next to you.

Golly, you appeared quickly this time, darling. Perhaps you fancy me. Shall I confuse you by ordering absinthe? Absinthe makes the parts grow longer, but I've given all that up. If you're after my body, lady, forget it. Whisky. How kind.

Is it my latent paranoia, or are people beginning

to stare at me as if I had three nostrils, cloven hooves and a forked tail? Am I the centre of interest among these dreary slobs? Parchment-faced commuters wondering when their lives are going to begin. A dosser on the scrounge. A lapsed intellectual in fluorescent socks. A woman with a beard. A tall, immaculately dressed civil servant haranguing a party of four. ("A camel may be a horse designed by a committee, old boy, but a camel is a bloody useful animal.") It's bad enough being a servant, old boy, without having to be civil as well. A trendy young man displaying his hairy chest to a bemused young nymphet who isn't even listening as he talks about "Vegas" and "LA" when the farthest west he has been is Wales. A dope-dealer drinking beer, a whore past her prime, a soldier between postings, a lonely clerk reluctant to go home. **This is life?**

Hearken, fellow humans, to the miscreant in your midst. A child is dying out there.

Camilla undresses in the back room and lies back nervously on a rubber sheet. The ex-midwife bustles in. She carries towels, pins, a bucket and a syringe. Camilla stares at the syringe. It's the safest way, dear. No incisions, no fear of infection. Nothing to worry about at all. Camilla, white-faced, can't speak. Naked from the waist down as if she is about to produce a beautiful baby, she feels exposed, vulnerable, humiliated, dirty.

She closes her eyes and wishes she was dead.

Enough. Must get to the loo. Use legs alternately. Ingenious these humans. Stop bumping into people. People don't like it.

Tears were streaming down his cheeks before he could reach the sanctuary of the lavatory, but it was only after he got there that his crying became noisy: he thought that he would choke.

Cool, wet tiles against his cheek told him that he was lying on the floor but he didn't remember how he got there. People milled around him now, more and more of them, moving his head to another more comfortable angle, staring at his tear-drenched face.

Somebody said: "Call an ambulance."

Oliver Oswald was short, dark and heavy. He was overweight in every department—his nose, his ears, his lips were all slightly fatter than you would expect in an admittedly plump man, as though someone had jammed the nozzle of a bicycle pump into an unspecified orifice and blown him up a little. He had a high, flat forehead with his rapidly receding black hair greased back like a man from the 1940s, an impression that was strengthened by his dark blue double-breasted suit. He was in his late thirties but looked ten years older, as if decay had already started. Galloping alopecia was rendering his comb redundant and, he would tell you proudly, proliferating piles had wreaked such havoc on his anus that he was now farting in E major. Oswald owned three garages in the town but, more surprisingly, was one of the few Socialist members of the County Council. His Socialism baffled those who knew him: Fred was convinced that he was really a crypto-Fascist, working for the overthrow of the Socialist ideal.

Three years earlier, as middle-age raced in, he had married a very young girl very quickly, and the romance was a rich source of gossip in a community that lived for it. He had found himself judging a beauty contest in London and he had fallen for the youngest contestant, a teenage student called Trixie. Trixie had only come third but Oliver thought her very beautiful and gave her a little clap. The following day, in the back of one of his cars, she returned the compliment but he took the penicillin manfully and married her within a month. Their relationship now reminded Fred of a couple of sky-divers whose parachutes have become lethally intertwined so that they fight and scream and kick at each other during the short spell of life that is left to them. The best that could be said about their affair was that at least two other lives weren't being ruined.

The trouble had begun early on with Oliver's inability to make the act of love last longer than a minute. He took advice, read a few books, and replaced the Oswalds' four-poster with a single bed on each side of which he placed a bucket of cold water. When he felt that he was about to ejaculate, he plunged his hands into each bucket. The trick worked: Oliver didn't come. But the practical consequences, apart from a ruined watch and a damp bed, were to permanently alienate Trixie, whose own private journeys were brought to a soggy and abrupt halt when her partner's cold, wet hands involuntarily grabbed her warm and busy buttocks. By way of compensation, a contrite Oliver invited his wife on their first wedding anniversary to write down the three things she would most like to do. He was making a lot of money and he wanted to pamper her. As an exercise, he wrote down the three things that he most wanted to do, and he hoped that some items on their lists would coincide.

He wrote:
1 Cross the Atlantic in Concorde and drive across America.
2 Go on a round-the-world cruise.
3 Buy a holiday-home abroad.

She wrote:
1 Screw Warren Beatty.
2 Snort cocaine.
3 Get a divorce.

Her replies affected Oliver deeply. He began to look like a man who had bought a car with no engine. The marriage started to fray. Oliver Oswald, husband, became a master of duplicity, making secret phone calls, hiding clean clothes at the office, removing only the lip-sticked cigarettes from his car's ashtray instead of alerting Trixie by emptying the whole box.

"Wotcha, Oliver," Dermot said to him.

"Dermot, Fred," Oliver Oswald said. "Where have you been? Have a drink?"

Fred selected his question. "Thanks."

"Funny thing, drinking," said Oliver, producing a five-pound note from the top pocket of his jacket. "Heavy drinking makes you fat, but excessive drinking causes malnutrition. I must concentrate on it a little more—I'm at the unattractive fat stage."

"You're one of these power merchants," Dermot told him. "Why can't we have the bars open all day like the continentals?"

"We're not like the continentals, that's why. I mean, what's the point of being German if you can't drink all day?"

Oliver Oswald was a patriot who believed in the old chauvinism—"Fog In Channel: Continent Isolated." He bought them each a British pint.

"How is Trixie?" Fred asked. Pints cost politeness.

"She phoned me up at work this morning just to give me an angry silence. I thought that was going a bit far. How is your lovely lady? A woman of mesmerising splendour."

"It's over," said Fred.

"Don't tell him that," said Dermot. "He'll be round there like a stoat."

"Why not?" asked Oliver Oswald. "I've had my eye on Camilla for some time."

"I noticed."

"Sort of thing you must expect if you go out with beautiful girls like that. Where is she? Where have you been? Did you tell me?"

"No, I didn't tell you," Fred said. Oliver not only looked oily, he sounded oily, as if he had used some rich garage lubricant on his throat. The idea of him pairing up with Camilla was more than Fred's imagination could manage.

Oliver Oswald shook his head slowly. "Do you think that sperm contains an irritant that makes you want to get rid of it?"

"An interesting concept, councillor."

"There's something funny going on down there. I've never been able to figure it out."

Fred left the two of them and went over to the jukebox near the door. Without further encouragement, perhaps Oliver would forget his curiosity about Camilla, even his obsession with girls.

A lady called Lolita was singing a song called "Amor, Amor"; it sounded like the authentic noise of female distress. His own taste in pop music was so unfashionable that he only dared use the jukebox when there were several records in the pipeline. That way nobody knew who to blame. He scanned the titles but he knew neither the artists nor the songs. With most of the records he couldn't even tell which was which (was it Fungus by Turds, or Turds by Fungus?). The new wave of pale and effete young men who wore eye make-up, puckered their lips, covered their acne with sequins and waved their bums at the cameras had driven him away from popular music a long time ago.

"A friend of mine's father practically owns Gibraltar," said a small girl with huge spectacles at the side of the jukebox. Her friend nodded, impressed. The tenuous link and the preposterous lie were absorbed into the hubble bubble of bar-room conversation. On his other side a tall young man with a very short haircut and a thick black moustache was being put down with some style by a hard-faced girl who looked as if she had already received enough propositions for one lifetime. He was trying to win the girl's interest, but his conversation would not come alive. "Do you know Brighton, at all?" he asked politely. "Here," she said, "are you what they call a charismatic verbaliser?"

Fred looked round the crowded room. This had once been a regular haunt of Camilla's on Saturday mornings, but there was no sign of her today. He wandered back through the gin and bitter lemon set to buy Trader Ryan and Oliver Oswald a drink.

"The opiate of the masses," Oliver Oswald was saying.

"I happened to mention that there is some interesting sport on television this afternoon," Dermot told Fred. "It seems that sport makes the councillor angry."

"I speak as a socialist," said Oliver Oswald, "not as a councillor."

"Well, it's your lot that goes to the cup final," said Fred. "They find it more interesting than your party political broadcasts."

"Not my point," said Oliver Oswald. "If they weren't so interested in whether Manchester United won they might get round to asking why Lord Thing had inherited seven thousand acres."

"Instead of which they are fully occupied kicking each other's heads in at football matches," said Dermot. "Is that what you liberated the working classes for?"

Oliver Oswald laughed. "There have been some negative aspects to the socialist revolution, I agree," he said. "Who wants a drink?"

"I'll get them," said Fred. He waited at the bar to get Miranda's attention. The crowds were drinking today as if prohibition started tomorrow. Where was the money shortage that the newspapers kept talking about?

He bought two pints of lager and a whisky for Oliver Oswald and as he turned round with the drinks Camilla came in. She gazed round the bar until she spotted him and came straight over. She looked even prettier than he had remembered, dressed today in a white roll-neck sweater and pale blue jeans.

"Where the hell have you been?" she said. "Where did you get to? What happened?"

"Christ, you look good," he told her. "Are you all right? Was everything all right?"

"I'm fine. Are you going to buy me a drink?"

"I certainly am."

He beckoned to Miranda again. By the time that he had bought Camilla a fruit juice—thinking, as he bought it, that his nerves were in a pretty jumpy state—Oliver Oswald and Trader Ryan had drifted the couple of yards across the carpet that was necessary to bring them into Camilla's orbit.

"How nice to see you again," said Dermot. "Have you been on holiday?"

"I have, actually," said Camilla. "A couple of weeks in Cornwall."

Fred gave her the drink. His hand was shaking.

"You are the very girl I wanted to see, my dear," said Oliver Oswald. "This town is looking for a carnival queen. It's the carnival soon and we're holding a contest to find a carnival queen. You must enter."

"Sorry," said Camilla. "I don't like that sort of thing."

"Shame," said Dermot.

"I don't know how girls can compete with each other in that way, parading in front of judges like dogs at Crufts."

She had always been shy in a crowd but today she had a new confidence. Fred watched her, impressed.

"It wouldn't be like that," said Oliver Oswald hastily. "I'm on the committee that's organising it. You wouldn't have to wear a bathing costume or anything like that. Look, supposing I bet you a hundred pounds that you wouldn't enter?"

Camilla looked doubtful. "What does that mean?"

"It means that he would give you a hundred pounds if you did enter," said Fred.

"Even if I didn't win?"

Oliver Oswald nodded.

"Okay," said Camilla. She turned to Fred. "Will he pay?"

"Gambling debts are always paid around here," he told her. "Usually by me."

"Well, it's good to see you two together again," said Oliver Oswald.

Camilla didn't say anything, and neither did Fred. There was a lot of explaining to do and no opportunity to do it. Customers milled around them, calling for drinks. Saturday evenings were being planned by people for whom Saturday evening was the only truly happy moment of the week. Voices bayed and brayed against a background of laughter and breaking glasses.

Camilla said: "I called at your flat several times."

"I only got back last night."

"Where from?"

"He won't tell us," said Dermot. "He ain't talking."

She looked at him questioningly to say, won't you tell me either?

But what could he tell her? That he had cracked? That he had been in a mental hospital for five weeks? It wasn't the sort of behaviour that captured the hearts of young ladies, it wasn't even something that you could talk about—despite the fact that more than 200,000 people in Britain did it every year. The public picture of the private misery still included blood chilling screams, unaccountable violence, dribbling maniacs and dirty straitjackets.

"Come round for lunch," he suggested. "I get very chatty over salmon salad."

His lager was already finished: he drank more quickly when he was nervous.

Camilla smiled. "Okay. I'll go and buy a bottle of wine. See you at the flat."

"There you go," said Dermot, when she had gone. "It's on again."

Outside, thc police were leading a little old man to a police car. The event had attracted quite a crowd.

"What did he do?" Fred asked a woman who was watching from a bus queue.

"He was singing," said the woman. "He wouldn't stop singing. Meths drinker, I expect."

Fred stumbled off, cheerful enough to break into a

few verses himself. Better not do that, though. Singing happily in the street? You can't do that there here.

Of course, if he had been crying in the street nobody would have taken any notice.

"After you left me at Paddington Station," said Fred an hour later, lying on the floor of his flat, "I went into the bar and had a few drinks. Perhaps I had too many drinks—I was feeling pretty depressed. Anyway, to get to the loo in this joint you had to go down a dozen stone steps, two of which I missed and ten of which I fell down. I banged my head on something and was out cold. They took me to hospital with concussion and I was there for five days trying to remember who I was. The doctors wouldn't let me leave hospital if I lived alone, so I went down to Dover to stay with my mother. It turns out that knocks on the head can be very dangerous things."

He had invented the story while walking back from the Cellar and he was rather proud of it.

"How extraordinary," said Camilla. "There was an ambulance leaving Paddington as we got back. I never imagined that you were in it."

"I was, though," he said, grateful that there was something that he could be truthful about.

Camilla sat in an armchair, a glass of red wine in her hand, looking down at him.

"Why didn't you write or phone? I mean, afterwards?"

He couldn't tell her why he hadn't written; it would sound too weak. Still, he was good at making up stories today. He said: "I was angry. I didn't want you to have an abortion. I saw it as a rejection of me. I still do."

"I'll never have another—never."

"Was it bad?"

"It was next day. The most awful stomach ache that you can imagine."

"I can imagine. That's my trouble."

He levered himself up on to one elbow and reached

across for his own wine. A brilliant sunshine was flooding the table in the middle of the room where their empty plates lay, along with a wooden salad bowl, half-eaten bread rolls and a now empty bottle of Chateau La Pierre Levée.

Camilla got up and joined him on the floor. "It wasn't a rejection of you, Fred. It was just something that had to be done. I haven't stopped thinking about you since that night."

Fred closed his eyes and realised that he was frightened. He was frightened of the power that she had over him, of the mess that she could quite easily make of his life. He had spent an entire evening in the Unit thinking about this, and discussing it with whoever would listen. He had concluded that he had a better chance of staying whole without her. He was too vulnerable to her, too exposed emotionally. I can't handle it, he told himself in the jargon of the patients. She could pick him up, play with him, and throw him away without a second thought, and he would be back in the Unit, fingering his scar tissue.

He decided that night not to write to her, nor to contact her when he got out. But, he had to admit now, if she came to him he was incapable of sending her away.

He looked across at her, he imagined, much as a rabbit looks at a snake.

"Have you got a job?" he asked.

"I've applied for one. Air hostess. But I don't even get an interview for weeks. That hundred pounds from Mr Oswald will come in handy." She bent over and kissed him. "Shall we go to bed? It's been a long time."

"Do you mind if we don't?" he said. "I'm not that bright today."

She looked down at him.

"Don't you love me any more?"

"Oh yes," he said sadly.

"That's good. I love you, too."

It was the first time that she had said it. She stood up and returned to her armchair. "I've got to rather like sex. With you, I mean."

He imagined her naked body wriggling beneath his and it did nothing to him. Since his collapse he had experienced no sexual feelings at all. For a moment he was seriously worried. Was it an illness? Had some physical defect appeared to kill all passion? Or was it a psychological result of the abortion, a deep fear of another pregnancy?

"It's not just my body you want, is it?" he said. "I've got a mind, too, you know."

Camilla laughed. "I hope your luminous watch hasn't impaired your virility."

"No, I wear it round my wrist."

He continued lying on the floor feeling strangely listless. A profound interest in the opposite sex was what had kept him going this far—that and an ability to delude himself about his prospects. Perhaps he would have to revert to the dietary experiments of his youth when he spent weeks scouring the shelves of the supermarkets for aphrodisiacs. He remembered discovering that after enough lettuce even the words "physically aroused" aroused him physically.

The memory of the boost that lettuce had given him goaded him to his feet. "Let's get out into that sunshine, and I'll buy you a present."

She hugged herself like a happy child. "Lovely! Buy me an album."

They went downstairs and into the street to mingle with the busy, Saturday afternoon shoppers who smiled and laughed their way from one store to the next.

Fred kept one eye on them all the time. The human race is incredible, he thought. People whose presence on this planet followed nothing more calculated than a spontaneous act of lust by two other people go out, make friends, laugh and enjoy themselves, behaving for all the world as if they have **chosen** to be here!

Three

> Most people are too busy earning
> a living to make any money.
> **Racing advertisement**

The idea that gambling was his magic ticket to survival came to Fred one afternoon as he read the papers in a coffee bar in the town. It was small, poorly lit and inadequately ventilated, and the stench of stale sweat, mingled with cheap scent, hung on the air like a fog, but a strong black coffee and an even stronger cigarette made him oblivious of the local discomforts. He saw the truth starkly, as Paul saw the truth on the road to Damascus: judgment and commonsense could turn one pound into two pounds without going to work. It was the idea that he had been looking for.

He turned to the racing pages of the paper and began to devise a method of investing on the horses that would show a profit even if only one horse in four won; it was simply a question of adjusting his stake to accommodate previous losses and possible starting prices. All he needed was an occasional winner and even a child with a pin had to find some winners. He ran his eye down the list of the day's runners and chose four horses on their past form. The horses that he picked had won before; he ignored those that hadn't.

The betting shop next door was a miserable place with its linoleum floor, fluorescent lighting and cheap, uncomfortable stools; gambling was legal in Britain, but you were not supposed to enjoy it as well. The racing pages from the daily newspapers covered the walls and half a dozen gamblers stood around with betting slips in their hands, their optimism stoically concealed.

Fred pulled a betting slip from a container on the wall and wrote down the name of his first horse. It was expected to start at two to one and he put five pounds on it. It started at six to four and came fifth. His second horse was expected to be an even bet. He put ten pounds on it. A pale girl in dark glasses took his money, clock-timed his receipt and returned the slip, carrying out the whole operation without uttering a word. He pulled a stool up against the wall and listened to the crackling of the blower. The results of races at four meetings were being relayed to the glum punters who were now starting to fill the shop. Fred began to wonder whether gambling was quite what he was looking for if it had this demoralising effect on the participants.

The second horse lost by seven lengths, the blower told him. He was unmoved. His third horse seemed likely to start at a better price. It was called The Trader. Fred put eight pounds on it and paid the tax on the stake, which would be better than paying it on his winnings.

An old lady shuffled in nervously with her housekeeping. Punters who had lost peered at the pages on the wall for hope.

The girl in dark glasses and the shop manager beside her kept their heads down as the money flowed in their direction. You never saw a bookie in a bus queue.

It was a seven-furlong race for two-year-olds, a guide to next year's classics, said the newspaper on the wall. The Trader won at five to one in a photo-finish.

Fred collected his forty pounds winnings as if it happened every day. He had made a profit of twenty-five pounds in just over an hour. He walked out into the sunshine and wondered how the workers were getting on.

The future suddenly looked easy.

The following day he went to Goodwood—an activity that paid twenty-five pounds an hour deserved serious application. He became convinced that something dramatic was happening in his life. A method of gambling which eliminated the element of luck would provide comparative wealth quite quickly, and wealth would mask his problem or even cure it. After that, he told himself, he would go out gladly and find himself a job—an unpaid job where his efforts benefited those less fortunate than himself. The satisfaction which had escaped him so far would be his. First acquire wealth, and then practise virtue.

Goodwood was as glorious as its publicity said. The racecourse was tucked into the sweeping hills of the South Downs, and from one horizon to another you saw only the rolling fields and the trees: there was not a building in sight. The sky was an almost unnaturally deep blue.

Between the tall, white stand and the racetrack fifty yards in front, scores of bookmakers from all over the country had set up in business with a board, a box to stand on and a big leather bag for the money. It was these gentlemen who would shortly be dealing with Fred and he watched them for a while, wondering whose profits he should deplete. They in turn were watching the tic-tac men who were spaced out all the way down the course, signalling the starting-prices to the bookies. But only the bookies knew which horse they meant because of the twist: horse number one wasn't necessarily horse number one on the racecard—that was where the twist came in.

Fred went behind the stand to the paddock where the runners for the first race were being led round by youths from the stable. Top-hatted owners stood on the lawn in the middle, waiting to meet the jockeys. Given the money that owning a racehorse cost, they had paid dearly for their big moment.

The great Lester Piggott emerged, whip under arm, and shook hands with an unknown owner before strolling across the lawn to mount his horse. As he rode it slowly round the paddock, he turned his face away from anyone who tried to photograph him.

No horse in the first race gave Fred sufficient confidence to bet, and he walked back round the stand to enjoy it without the tension of financial involvement. Thousands of people were hurrying in front of the stand now, and every other one seemed to have a rolled-up newspaper in one hand and a pair of binoculars hanging from the neck. They went from one bookmaker to the next, comparing available prices.

All the horses except Piggott's galloped down to the start, which was a mile away over the hills and out of sight. Piggott's walked all the way. It came out of the starting-stalls last, according to the loud-speakers, and it was last when they came into the straight where the crowd could see them. As the field swept past the three-furlong marker, Piggott, bottom in air, swept past the field. He won by five lengths.

Fred went across to the narrow path that the horses had to use to get from the racetrack to the stables. Gambling was a serious business and he might learn something.

"Only one bloody pace," said a jockey to the

stable-lad who met him. "Never really got going," said another. The horses were steaming and the jockeys' faces were as red as laterite. Piggott said nothing.

Fred bought an ice-cream and wandered back to the bookmakers. His plan for the second race involved no cerebral activity at all beyond discovering the name of Piggott's mount. One bookmaker was offering four to one and he put ten pounds on it.

To Fred's surprise, the horse was unplaced. In the third race, a hot favourite from France was expected to win slowing down. It was a big black shiny animal that looked as if it could give a few lengths' start to a train. It was odds-on with all the bookmakers so Fred put thirty pounds on it and then sat on the grass in the sun and waited for affluence to arrive. Across the Downs the sun glinted on the roofs of thousands of cars parked in the fields. Around him pretty girls in summer dresses strolled languidly past, helplessly, hopelessly irresistible. Fred resisted them. This was work.

The big black horse from France lost to an outsider in a photo-finish. Fred hurried into the bar where a close-circuit television showed a re-run of each race. The horse had clearly won and then it had lost.

"Got a pebble up its bottom in the last furlong," said an old man carrying a shooting-stick.

Fred was undismayed. He only needed one winner and Piggott was obviously going to win the fourth race on an Irish horse that had never been beaten. The only problem would be the odds. He left the bar and studied the prices offered by more than forty bookmakers. A red-headed gentleman from the West Country was offering two to one. Fred pressed fifty pounds into his grateful hand, collected his ticket, and returned to the paddock to look at the horse. It was a big, bay colt that seemed to be laughing. Fred looked at Piggott. Piggott wasn't laughing. Fred was reassured.

Piggott took the horse gently down to the start, not walking this time, but not exerting himself either. The race, a five-furlong sprint, was run on the straight with the horses appearing suddenly over the brow of a hill soon after the start.

Fred stood on a seat and calmly watched the bay colt pound towards him. It was holding its head to one side which alarmed Fred but didn't seem to impede its speed. It was so far in front so quickly that Fred wondered whether the rest of the field could see it.

He threw his newspaper into a litter-bin. How could you lose if you stopped when you were winning?

"I made fifty pounds today," he told Dermot in the Cellar. "It beats going to work."

"Gambling is work," said Dermot. "Very draining, emotionally."

"I don't feel at all drained," said Fred. "It's just a matter of commonsense. What do they play in that casino up the road?"

"Roulette, blackjack, craps."

"Roulette sounds a good idea. Come up there and I'll show you how to make money."

"Something I've always wondered about," said Dermot.

They finished their drinks and left the bar. The summer sun had finally gone down but it was still light. Fred walked silently, dreaming up methods of winning at roulette.

People who went to Carlo's Casino out of a misguided longing for glamour or sophistication were surprised to find themselves in a one-storey building that was decently concealed in one of the town's side-streets. At the near end, as you went in, there was a bar, and in the middle of the room were several sofas and glass-topped tables with two huge fruit machines against the wall. The gambling was done at the far end of the room. Twenty or thirty people were standing or sitting round a French roulette table, another crowd was playing dice and a third group sat on high stools at the blackjack table where a dealer slid cards at high speed from a shoe on his left.

Dermot, a member of this as of any other club within ten miles, signed Fred in as a guest and they went over to the roulette.

Roulette was clearly not a cheerful game. The obvious misery of the two Italian croupiers was mirrored by the unhappiness of the gamblers. Compared with the people in here, the mournful mob in the betting shop were having the time of their lives. The faces stared, devoid of expression, the wheel span, the ball settled, the hearts sank.

A croupier raked chips from the table. "Place your bets, gentlemen," he said, an Italian running a French game in English. Fred looked round at the unsuccessful gamblers. Mostly they were young men, but there were several elderly married couples trying to work out where the ball was going to fall. Behind them Fred could see Oliver Oswald, standing alone, nervously scratching his teeth with his fingernails and muttering imprecations. He obviously didn't have a system.

Fred pulled the pile of notes from his back pocket and counted off a hundred pounds. He laid them on a corner of the table and had the croupier's instant attention.

"Ten pound chips," he said.

The rake removed the paper money and pushed ten white chips towards him. He left seven in front of him and put one chip on red and two on black. It had been red last time. The man sitting nearest to him began to smile when he saw what Fred had done.

"Hedging your bet?" asked Dermot.

Fred smiled as the croupier spun the wheel. The table was now covered with chips of different denominations, and the customers were hypnotised by the little ivory ball which rolled noisily round before settling in number eighteen, which was red. Fred replaced his winnings on red with one chip, but put four on black. The ball landed in twenty-two, which was black, so he put two chips on red and one on black. Three reds in a row followed, and by his sixth spin Fred had one chip on red and eight on black. Black won.

The man who had smiled when Fred placed his original bet had now stopped smiling—and gambling. He had been betting **en plein,** with **chevals** and **carres** to cover the neighbours of his number, but Fred's simple system suddenly had more appeal. He was automatically winning ten pounds every time the ball landed. After ten spins he had won a hundred pounds.

He cashed his chips and went to the bar. Dermot followed.

"I've won one hundred and fifty pounds today," said Fred. "I don't know how I'm going to make ends meet."

"You were lucky that zero didn't come up," said Dermot. "I've never seen anyone back black **and** red before."

"Zero wouldn't make any difference. You just adjust the stake. Have a very large gin."

Oliver Oswald came over.

"Care to lose some of that money playing poker, Fred?" he asked. "A few people are coming back to my place for a game."

"Why not? It's my lucky day," said Fred.

No optimism is less amenable to reason than the optimism of the gambler and, as they swept through the night in Oliver Oswald's Mercedes, Fred contemplated further additions to his growing capital.

There were four of them in the car besides Oliver: Fred, Dermot, Nick (a young Oswald employee), and Mr Johnson, a fat and jovial man who was a back-room official at the council that Oliver Oswald sat on. Both Nick and Mr Johnson referred to Oswald as Olly.

"What do you think of your beloved Labour Party now, then?" asked Mr Johnson, chuckling. "Three by-elections. Three defeats. The country hates you, Olly."

Oliver turned off the main road out of town and headed up the country lane that led to his enormous house. He drove carefully. A sticker on the car's rear window said: ARRIVE ALIVE.

"They wouldn't be voting Conservative if it was a general election," he said. "They know they won't put the Tories in so they give themselves a thrill by kicking Labour at a piddling by-election. Pleasure without responsibility. All these bloody voters are doing is wanking in the polling booth."

Mr Johnson's huge frame shook with laughter on the front seat.

Oliver Oswald lived in a palace that was already famous. Even people who had never been there were familiar with his black bedroom, his new circular bed, his exotic plants and his fancy lights. The joke that travelled was that he had once covered the bedroom ceiling with mirrors and then found that he had to wear glasses in bed to enjoy it. The house had all the atmosphere of a **fin de siècle** brothel. When the foreign visitors of the twenty-first century arrived in their supersonic air-bubbles, Fred suspected, this is where the conducted tours would lead them. A dozen famous men who had lived and died in this town would be relegated to schoolkids' fodder; it was Oliver Oswald's sink of depravity that would bring the philistines flocking. Mr. Oswald, in his grave, would become one of Britain's invisible assets.

A wide oak staircase that curved away into the distance faced them as they came through the front door, the walls were dark and opaque, and the lights were red. Somewhere, Fred thought, there is probably a tower and a minstrels' gallery.

Oliver led them into a large room downstairs that was strangely modern: satinwood carpets, small onyx tables, the best contemporary furniture. Fred picked up a book that lay on one of the tables. It was called **Shin Buddhism.** Oliver was full of surprises.

The host disappeared and reappeared with a tray containing five glasses, two bottles of gin, an ice container, and a roll of green baize which he laid over the largest table in the room.

"Sit down, gentlemen," he said. "Sit down and get your money out."

Mr Johnson poured himself a gin.

"Where is Mrs Oswald?" he said.

Oliver produced a pack of cards. "In bed with her vibrator, I imagine. I hope it shakes the legs off the bloody bed." He began to shuffle the cards.

"Olly's got birds that Trixie hasn't heard about," said Nick cheerfully. He was wearing a yellow roll-neck sweater, and he chewed gum with his mouth open to emphasise his simple masculinity.

"They're getting too young for me," said Oliver. "They make demands on my private parts that I'm unable to meet. And all that chat you have to put up with!"

"What you need," said Dermot, "is a photostat of your small-talk. You just hand it to them and say, 'Here's my small-talk. Read that. If you like it, we can get on with the serious stuff.'"

"I haven't got any small-talk," said Mr Johnson. He had removed his jacket and was revealing a pair of bright red braces. He was also revealing, Fred noticed, bodily secretions of awesome pungency. "You mustn't regard yourself as old, Olly," he said. "It's self-fulfilling."

"I **am** old," said Oliver Oswald. "My God, I can remember when you could take off your trousers without taking your shoes off first."

"And now you fancy Fred's girl, I hear," said Mr Johnson. "What are you going to do about that?"

"I'm open to suggestions. Preferably improper ones. What is that Fred's got, Dermot? What's his secret?"

"Charisma," said Dermot, "with a capital fucking K."

"What do you do, Fred?" asked Mr Johnson, turning to look at the subject of this conversation. "What's your job?"

Fred took a large sip of gin. "I'm a prison governor," he said.

"There are more people in prison today than at any time in this century," said Mr Johnson. "Did you know that?"

He sounded drunk already, and Fred hoped fervently that he was.

"I had five women in one weekend once," said Nick, evidently feeling neglected.

"Why only five?" said Oliver Oswald.

"The splint broke," said Dermot.

Oliver continued shuffling the cards and then stopped to pour himself a large gin. "Five-card stud poker," he announced. "Stripped pack, sevens upwards. One card down, four up. Okay?"

"Righto," said Mr Johnson, getting out his wallet. They put some money in front of them, and Oliver dealt them all two cards, one facing down, one facing up.

Fred—casually studying the opulence of the room—remembered hearing how Oliver had begun to accumulate his wealth. He had bought cars in Scotland and sold them in London where they were worth two hundred pounds more. His natural talent for dissembling should make him a formidable poker-player.

His up card was a king, the highest card showing, so he opened the betting with a pound note which he placed in a wooden bowl at the centre of the table.

Dermot threw in a pound as well, but Fred, who had a queen up and a hidden seven, passed his hand without betting. He passed several hands until he got two aces "back to back" and opened the betting with a pound. His third card was an ace as well, and he bet four pounds but the others passed. He counted his winnings on the pot: three pounds. What you needed was a hand that was good but didn't look so good that it frightened the others off.

After half an hour Fred had lost ten pounds through betting a pound when he had a likely first pair and then passing because he didn't like his third card. It won't do, he thought. He was there to make money. After drinks in the Cellar and more at the casino he was surprisingly sober; concentration and a little luck should enlarge his capital tonight. He sipped his neat gin thoughtfully.

Mr Johnson was enjoying himself, neither risking nor losing too much, but treating the whole evening as if it were a civilised game of bridge. Nick played tensely, his jaw working on the gum, his eyes shooting round the table, watching the cards as soon as they arrived. Dermot played morosely, as if card games were a conversation-killing bore. Oliver was the happiest, betting more recklessly than the others and winning more often as his large bets discouraged opposition.

"I've nearly done my bin, kiddo," said Dermot, looking at the money in front of him.

"How much have you lost?" Fred asked.

"Twenty-five. I've got another tenner and that's it."

"Your bets aren't big enough to work," said Oliver Oswald. "You're as tight as a goat-herd's hand-drum."

"Tight? I give till it hurts. My old lady will murder me."

"If she complains, belt her," said Oliver, fanning the cards over the table. "Seven hundred million people are living in destitution tonight. You capitalists don't know how lucky you are."

The remark raised a small laugh. Fred scowled. If

Oliver Oswald had been a fascist, it would have been a lot easier to understand.

"What the hell are you a socialist for, anyway, Oliver?" he said. "I've never understood it, considering the tax you must pay." He pulled a fat cigar from a packet that was provided for guests and lit with Oliver's gold lighter. He didn't enjoy cigars much, but perhaps they would aid concentration.

Oliver smiled benignly. "To each according to his need, from each according to his ability. That's socialism. If you don't like it go and live somewhere else. I do like it."

"There's less competition for a Labour seat on the council round here," said Mr Johnson, winking. "Olly wanted to be a celebrity."

Fred didn't see Oliver as a celebrity, but others did. He remembered when he and Dermot had decided to form a lunch club. It was to meet once a month at the best French restaurant in the town, and they were each to bring one guest to the table. The choice of guests decided who would pay the bill. One month the competition would be to see who could bring the most boring guest. The one who did had a free lunch. Another month they were going to see who could bring the guest with the biggest breasts. Fred suggested that they could also try to produce a celebrity each, but Dermot said that the only celebrity they knew was Oliver Oswald and he didn't fancy that. Oliver Oswald was not Fred's idea of a celebrity.

At two o'clock Mr Johnson suggested that they should play the last hand.

Oliver gave the pack a special, long shuffle and shot them each two cards.

"What have we here?" said Mr Johnson. "A box of jewels or a can of worms?"

"Ring the Lutine bell," said Dermot.

"I'm not all that tickled with it," said Mr Johnson.

Fred showed a king. He tipped the corner of his

down card: it was another king. He put one card on top of the other in case there were any secret marks on the back, and looked round the table. Dermot had an eight, Mr Johnson a ten, but both Oliver and Nick had aces.

"If this is the last hand, let's make it a pot to remember," said Oliver, putting a five-pound note into the wooden bowl.

Nick and Fred pushed five-pound notes across the table, but Dermot and Mr Johnson passed.

"I'm surrounded by fools and idiots," said Oliver. "You'll never make money that way."

He dealt the third card. Fred received a queen but both Oliver and Nick had been dealt another ace. Nick began to look like a golfer who had holed his tee shot.

"I don't think anybody is going to get three aces round here," Fred told him. I, on the other hand, could easily get three kings, he thought. None has appeared elsewhere. Good thinking, Edward G.

"Unlikely, Fred," said Oliver. "I'll still bet ten pounds."

Nick and Fred each handed over a ten-pound note.

Oliver's fourth card was a seven, Nick's was a queen and so was Fred's: he had two pairs—was a full house on the way?

"Very interesting," said Oliver. "I wonder if Fred has three queens?"

"It's worrying, isn't it?" said Fred.

Nick bet ten pounds, but Oliver raised it to twenty.

"There's one hundred and five pounds in the pot so far," he said, "and still one card to come."

Fred began to feel nervous as Oliver picked up the cards. A king or a queen would win him the pot—Oliver's pot to remember. He stared expressionlessly at the card that came towards him. It was a seven.

Nick had a seven, too. Oliver had a queen.

"Three sevens showing," said Dermot, watching.

"More important are four queens," said Oliver. "Don't think Fred has three, after all."

Fred drank his gin and didn't say anything. It was the type of hand that he dreaded: he was fairly certain that he had won—sure enough to bet a lot of money if he had to—but he could not be quite certain. He studied the four cards that were showing in front of each player.

Oliver: two aces, a seven, a queen.

Nick: two aces, a queen, a seven.

Fred: a king, two queens and a seven with a king in the hole to make two pairs. Neither of his opponents could have three aces, nor could they have a pair of queens, and three sevens were showing.

"Check," said Nick.

"Fifty pounds," said Fred, but Oliver wasn't frightened.

"And raise it fifty," he said quickly.

"Muchas gracias," said Nick, and turned his cards down.

Fred's heart began to race as Oliver counted a hundred pounds into the bowl. Should he throw in the extra fifty pounds to see Oliver's cards, raise the bet still further, or quit? He checked his down card again to reassure himself that he really did have a pair of kings and a pair of queens, and then he looked at the cards in front of Oliver and considered the possibilities again. He couldn't have three aces, all four had been seen. He couldn't have a pair of queens, Fred had two and Nick had the fourth. Three sevens were showing.

He decided quickly: Oliver was trying to bully him with money. Well, he had chosen the wrong man. Fred had money at the moment. He was also, as of today, a highly successful gambler.

He took in about a litre of air, and said: "I'll raise it the pot."

Oliver emptied the bowl on the table and began to

count the notes. Fred already knew that there was two hundred and fifty-five pounds in it.

"Plus fifty pounds to meet my raise," said Oliver. "Call it three hundred pounds."

A clucking of tongues and a sucking of teeth came from the non-combatants.

Fred produced his roll of notes, twenties, tens and fives, and counted off three hundred pounds. Oliver put it in the bowl and stared at it. Fred stared at it, too—three hundred and eighty-five pounds of the money there was his.

The silence rolled on. Oliver blew his nose forcefully and then studied the contents of his handkerchief.

For a few moments, while Oliver went through the silent ritual of consideration, Fred thought that he had won, that Oliver would quit and push the bowl of money towards him. But suddenly he was reaching into an inside pocket for a fat leather wallet.

"I'll meet that and raise it five hundred pounds," he said quietly. He laid a wad of twenty-pound notes on the table and began to count.

Fred said quickly: "Well, I don't have five hundred pounds."

"You can owe it," said Oliver. "Your credit's good. Now I owe seven hundred and fifty pounds. I'm putting in thirty-eight twenty-pound notes and taking out a tenner. Okay?"

"Jesus," said Dermot. "I thought we were all supposed to be bankrupt in this country." He gazed enviously at the kitty.

Fred gazed at it, too. Oliver's big bet had convinced him that he was trying to frighten him with money and that he didn't have the winning hand. If his cards were winners he would have bet less to encourage Fred to stay in the game and lose a little more money.

Suddenly Oliver's face lit up.

"I'll tell you what I'll do if you don't want to run up a bill for five hundred quid. A rather unusual proposition. I've just put in five hundred pounds. You've got to put in something. I don't want money. I've got money."

Fred looked at him in confusion.

"What do you want?"

"A night with Camilla."

Fred gaped. The modesty of the request astonished him.

"All right," he said, and turned over his card. "Two pairs."

"Very good," said Oliver Oswald, studying them. "Very good indeed. But not good enough, I'm afraid." He turned his other card over. It was a seven. His two pairs had beaten Fred's two pairs. There had to be another seven somewhere—but why there?"

"Tough," said Dermot.

Fred felt sick but he forced himself to grin.

Louis the Fourteenth grinned, he thought, as the executioner held up his severed head.

Four

> The mass of men lead lives of quiet desperation.
> I am convinced that to maintain oneself on this
> earth is not a hardship but a pastime if we will
> live simply.
> **Thoreau**

Quite early the following morning, but not before most people had started work, Fred crept from the flat like a wounded cat and headed haltingly for the Cellar Bar. His mind was numbed by the events of the night before and by the lack of sleep that had followed them, and the brightness of the sun deceived him about the time: when he reached the Cellar's door it was still shut. He loitered impatiently on the pavement, like a man controlled by his thirst, and then wandered along to the newsagent to buy some papers. At this hour there would be no one to talk to in the Cellar.

When he returned, it was open. Miranda, standing on a tall stool, was opening a few of the high windows. He gazed at her thighs dispassionately, and picked a corner stool at the counter.

"Some happy juice, please, darling," he said.

Miranda slipped behind the bar and pulled him a pint of bitter. "You drink too much, Fred. You know that?"

"The one flaw in an otherwise saintly character, dear."

He opened his newspaper to see what other people were finding to do with their time. In Bermuda, a rich young couple with show-business and aristocratic connections were wondering whether to continue their honeymoon on safari in Kenya, or fly direct to Gstaad for the ski-ing. Life was full of difficult decisions like that. At Divonne-les-Bains, near the Swiss border, thirty-four uncommonly fit young men were about to devote the week to competing for a twenty-eight-thousand-pound golf prize. Meanwhile, in the north of England, bored teenagers were brightening their lives by hurling live cats down lift shafts, and in Battersea, a man who had gone into a public house to commit suicide had poured cyanide into his drink, picked up the wrong glass, and got five years for killing the barmaid. It was good to know that the rest of them were finding **something** to do.

He drank more than half his pint, and told Miranda: "The life-support system is malfunctioning."

She was squatting on the floor, restocking empty shelves with bottled beer.

"Some people go to work," she said.

"Well any fool can go to work! Surviving without it is a much more subtle manoeuvre."

Miranda stood up. "Work banishes those three great evils, boredom, vice and poverty."

"Which lunatic said that?"

"Voltaire."

"Oh."

You never knew with barmaids these days, he thought. Just as you were about to help them with the change, you discovered that they'd got a double first at Cambridge and were working here for fun.

"Most people need the daily dash of adrenalin provided by work," said Miranda, wiping the bar. She seemed unable to stay still. "Have you noticed how many people die quickly once they've retired? You ought to do something."

He finished his pint and pushed the empty glass towards her. He was tired—his eyes felt like footballs. "It's not what you do, it's what you are," he said. "I thought adrenalin was something you put on your hair?" There was no answer. "Anyway, you're quite wrong. Work isn't a natural instinct, it's an acquired habit. It's something that civilisation has inflicted on us. Animals don't work, you know. They eat, and screw, and kip, and that."

"Work is the reality," said Miranda firmly, handing him his drink.

"Well, I cross the street if I see reality approaching," said Fred.

"So I notice."

He despaired of finding support in this quarter, and decided to do some calculations on the back of his cigarette packet to see where he stood—or lay—financially. He had lost about four hundred pounds playing poker, not counting the five hundred pounds which Oliver Oswald would soon be looking for. But he had won eighty-five pounds on the horses and a hundred at roulette. With what was left from Mrs Saunders' present, he had about two hundred pounds. In a few days he had managed to dissipate a nest-egg which might have sustained him for months.

Miranda and the calculations made him turn reluctantly to the jobs advertisements in his paper. Was it conceivable that something here, a beautifully dressed-up offer of solid work—stunning prospects, an entire lifetime organised by a couple of sentences—would hook him, excite him, have him buying expensive notepaper for his sparkling letter of application? His eye ran down the page. The ever-increasing number of ways that strident or glib young men could earn a fat living didn't surprise him any more: work seemed to expand to accommodate the latest avalanche of phoneys, changing their names for the battle from Brian to Bryan, Nick to Nik, John to Jon. "Advertising copy-writer wanted." Slick phrase to sell the unwanted. "Is the onus on your anus? Make friends with your enema." What kind of background shot you anxious and panting into a job like that?

WHAT DO YOU WANT?

A good salary, security, status. . . . ? We start you at a salary of £8,000 and two years later a salary of £12,000 is the rule. Other benefits, of the same tenor, are better considered in context. What do we want? Those who are looking for an opportunity to build a new career so absorbing and rewarding that salary is soon of secondary importance. Men whose horizons can be extended because they have the imagination and the ability to cope. Those who can show us that they have the necessary substance to match their desire to be successful. Those who will be the basis of our future executive.

The possibility of somebody actually wanting to answer an advertisement like that sent a gust of depression through him. He turned to the others. Personnel managers were greatly in demand, but what was a personnel manager? What was a corporate planner? What was an entrepreneurial manager? What was a systems analyst? What was a process researcher, a marketing manager, or a slag chemist? Would you like to become an archivist in Zambia, a land surveyor in Malawi or a cartographer in the Caribbean?

No wonder he was jobless—he hadn't heard of half of these splendid occupations, let alone got a semblance of an idea how they were done, what was involved. What was that world outside of contributory pensions and tax-free emoluments, incrementals and differentials? What was this nervous pursuit of egalitarian affluence?

He knew, as he sat there, that he had never become involved with it because he had thought that he could stay outside. But what on earth had he expected to save him from the rat pit? The football pools? A 1954 penny? A rich relative? A scheme to bottle moonbeams? Was optimism commensurate with ignorance? Because, paradoxically enough, doctor, although I am fundamentally the biggest pessimist this side of the Iron Curtain, I have been sustained, during the darker hours, by an optimism so wholly irrational as to verge on insanity.

He started to think about the jobs that he had held—a score of jobs with not a single common thread—to convince himself, if nobody else, that work was something that he could handle if necessary. He had done it quite often, earning and saving, earning and saving so that he could drop the burden when his bank account said so and revert to the leisured existence which evidently came more naturally to him than to anybody else. Those beautiful out-of-work periods would have lasted a lot longer without his patronage of the Cellar, but here he was, at it again, approaching the third pint, the pint of no return. Only closing time would shift him from his stool now, and closing time seldom found the job a pushover.

"Listen," he said to Miranda, "what sort of life are we all leading if we haven't time to sniff the roses?"

He handed her his empty glass.

"Very sensible ones, I should think," Miranda said, filling the glass. "I know a man who was killed because he sniffed roses."

"Killed?"

"He got an earwig lodged in his sinus cavity and it

worked its way up to his brain."

"Sniffing roses can seriously damage your health?" There was no end to the bad news.

"Life isn't about sniffing roses, Fred," said Miranda. "It's about work."

"If that's the case, I have a complaint to make. I'm not here on that condition. Nobody asked me. I wasn't consulted. What contract did I sign?"

"The complaints desk is closed."

He remembered clocking in to a tile factory in the dark hours of many a cold morning. (Law of employment: The more unpleasant the job, the earlier you start in the morning.) He stood from 7.30 until 5.30 at night at the end of a conveyor belt as the wet, newly made tiles came out of the factory. You discarded the broken ones and picked up the others, piling them neatly in fours before putting them on to another belt which took them across the yard. Ten hours a day, with half an hour for lunch, standing there alone, lifting tiles which never stopped coming, never stopped asking to be lifted. He had stuck that job for ten months. **Why don't you get a job, Fred**?

He remembered working in another factory, lifting wood on to a planing-machine. That was another start-in-the-middle-of-the-night job, clocking in at the time-machine and losing an hour's pay if you were five minutes late. And what was an hour's pay? He couldn't remember. The wood was piled up on one side of the machine, he lifted it on, adjusted the blade, trimmed the wood, lifted it off and started a fresh stack on the other side. Don't stop. Nobody stop. Keep the factory going. **Why don't you get a proper job, Fred**?

There was none of that trade-union nonsense in the factories where Fred had worked. The hours were long, the pay was low, productivity was high and the profits were enormous.

I have seen the past and it works.

He remembered working in a shop—nine o'clock

start this time and wear a suit. Be polite to the customers but on no account allow them to leave before they have bought something. If necessary, kick their legs from under them as they reach the doormat. He remembered three months as a petrol pump attendant. The bigger the car, the more they expected—none of this blowing up their own tyres. When the Bentleys cruised on to the forecourt you practically had to hold their handkerchiefs for them while they blew their noses, if not wipe their bottoms. He remembered helping to lay a tennis court in a month, during his career as a labourer, the hardest job of all and, consequently, the worst paid. (Law of employment: pay increases as work decreases.) He remembered driving a van for a grocer who was fighting a lonely war against the big supermarkets. Sixty loads of groceries, now find the sixty houses to match. He could even recall a brief interlude as a telephonist, shoving plugs in all the wrong sockets like a blind sex maniac. **Why don't you get a job, Fred?** He remembered the story about Bob Dylan, holed up in his flat writing songs for weeks on end until his worried friends asked him: "Why don't you go out, Bob?" and Dylan replying: "Man, I've been out."

He wished that he had been a Conservative. They had a much better life. He wished that he had been a Jew. They had money (Jesus Saves, Moses Invests). Yet when he thought of the millions and millions of pounds that were passing backward and forward all over the country every few minutes it didn't really seem difficult to deflect a little of it his way. But work wasn't the answer. All work ever got you was enough money to last until the following week so that you went in and worked again: body and soul hung together by a gossamer thread. Why should he be one of the rats in the pit, waiting for the trap-door to produce the biscuit? If you didn't work, you didn't starve. You didn't disappear in a puff of smoke.

He stumbled to the lavatory, noticing with

surprise that the bar had filled up whilst he had been wrestling, single-handed, with these weighty matters. The contraceptive machine in the men's had, according to a notice on it, been made to British Standard Specifications. Underneath this proud announcement somebody had written: So was the Titanic. Another secret writer had scribbled over the machine's coin entrance: Insert foetus here for refund!!!! Fred returned to the bar, grinning.

Among the new arrivals was Trader Ryan.

Something hilarious had happened to him and most of the bar was listening to his account of it. An Edwardian glazed bookcase had been advertised in the local newspaper that morning, and before most people had left their beds Dermot was striding up a long drive towards a big house in the country with a pocket full of money. A huge dog, "slightly larger than a horse", came bounding down the drive to meet him. It leaped up at him, keen to get its playful paws on his shoulders, anxious, apparently, to lick his face. Dermot, backing away, found himself pinioned to a brick wall—once it had got its paws on his shoulders, the dog was taller than he was. The window of an upstairs room flew open, and the booming, upper-class voice of the resident matriarch echoed across the lawns: "Kick his balls! Kick his balls!" Stunned by the advice but alarmed by the dog, Dermot managed to get sufficient leverage to aim a boot at the monster's reproductive equipment. "No, no, no!" shrieked the upper-class voice. 'His **tennis** balls!"

"Here we are again," he said, as Fred approached. "Glasses in hand, livers rotting." He turned to Miranda. "Have you met Cardboard Fred, manic depressive and **nouveau pauvre**?"

"How are you, Dermot?"

"Ploughing a bleak furrow. Recovered from your losses?"

"No, but things will improve."

"He said, scratching his malnutrition sores. It

was a stupid game for you to have played. You don't have the same control as you do with horses or roulette."

"Have a drink," said Fred.

Dermot nodded. "I think I'd better. That bitch wanted a ton for the bookcase. I'd have told her where to stick it if the dog hadn't been there." He climbed on to his usual bar stool and studied Fred intently. "What are you going to do about it?" he asked.

"Do?" said Fred. "About it?"

"Are you pissed?"

"I would be if you'd let me get us drinks. Miranda."

Foaming lager appeared.

"What am I going to do about what?"

"About your disastrous bet with Mr Oswald."

"Pay him. Eventually."

Dermot shook his head very slowly.

"He won't want money. You bet him a night with Camilla."

"A night out with Camilla, I believe it was. I'd sooner pay him."

"I think you've made a mistake there, kiddo. Oswald said a night with Camilla. He means sleep with her. He's not thinking of taking her to the pictures. He wants to give her one."

"Are you sure?"

"Absolutely."

"He must be mad."

"He's going to be mad with you if you don't understand what the gamble was. What on earth did you think he was putting up five hundred pounds against?"

"The pleasure of Camilla's company for an evening. I'm sure he said 'night out'."

Dermot started shaking his head again. "He did not. I was amazed that you accepted the bet."

"To tell you the truth, I was so certain that I'd won that I hardly listened."

"My original question, what are you going to do about it?"

Fred ran his fingers through the back of his hair. It was a nervous habit of recent origin.

"Well, I'm not about to ask Camilla to sleep with Oliver."

"Good. I'm glad to hear it."

"Jesus swept. Did you think I might?"

"All I know is that you don't have five hundred pounds."

Fred drank some lager and tried to recall the conversation at the poker table. He was confused by Dermot's interpretation of what had been agreed when the last hand of the evening lay like a time-bomb on the table. Confusion was joined by incredulity, and both replaced by anger.

"What a bastard that man is," he said eventually. "He thinks his money can buy anything."

"It can," said Dermot, "except happiness. Look at his marriage."

"No thanks."

"I don't think he's a man who would be prepared to wait too long for a debt to be settled. On the other hand, what can he do about it?"

"Quite a lot, I should think." Worrying over this, Fred discovered that his glass was empty. "I'll have something short," he said. "The main digestive tract is awash."

Dermot called to Miranda, now hectically busy with the lunchtime business. He handed Fred his drink and said: "The man himself has just come in. Grinning guiltily, like a monk with a hard-on."

Fred turned and saw Oliver beckoning him to a quiet corner of the room. He went over, taking his new drink with him.

"A word in your ear," said Oliver Oswald. He indicated, by glancing to each side, that this was between the two of them.

"If you're looking for five hundred pounds, Oliver, you could have picked a better week."

Oliver held up both hands, palms outwards.

"Five hundred pounds? Do I need five hundred pounds? That wasn't the bet, Fred."

"I seem to recall that five hundred pounds came into it somewhere."

"It came into it, all right. It came into it on my side. What you were offering was quite different. I staked five hundred pounds. Your stake was a night with Camilla. I was hoping you would remember."

Fred stared at his new drink and considered this. He discovered that he was having a gin with sugar, citric acid, saccharin, polymethyl siloxane and preservatives—gin and tonic it was called.

"I'll get the money," he said.

Oswald stood, shaking his head. "I don't want the money, Fred. I've got the money. I've got money coming out of my ears. I'm bored with money."

"And now you're going to get some more. It must be a drag, but I always pay my debts. People like me couldn't survive if we didn't."

Oswald stopped shaking his head and commenced nodding it.

"Quite, Fred. I'm sure you do. But the debt isn't money. And you have as much chance of finding five hundred pounds . . ."

"As you have of a night with Camilla."

Oswald leaned forward, elbow on bar, chin on palm.

"I don't think I like that much, Fred," he said quietly. "You played the game. You would have taken my five hundred pounds. But you lost. What is this? Are we all supposed to subsidise Cardboard Fred?"

"I've told you. You'll get your money."

"And I've told you. I don't want it. I want your doxy."

"My what?"

"Your doxy."

"Well, my doxy, as you call her, would be worth a lot more than five hundred pounds, if she were available. Which she isn't."

"Your valuation, Fred. Not mine. And don't tell me that she's not available. You offered her."

"I was drunk."

"Drunk or sober, a bet's a bet. I hope there's not going to be any welshing on this, and I'm not talking about five hundred pounds. Which I could have lost to you just like that."

Fred wanted to tell him that this wasn't true, that Oliver knew he had won before he made the bet because there was no card that Fred could have held which would have beaten two aces and two sevens. But he didn't say anything. This was one of those circular conversations that eventually delivered all involved back to their original starting-points. When you arrived there, you got off. But Oliver hadn't arrived yet.

"I fancy her, you see," he said, as if this aspect hadn't received sufficient emphasis. "I'd crawl over broken glass to lick it. You're going to honour this debt, Fred. Be sure of that."

He backed away and disappeared into the lunch-time drinkers.

A pink cnvelope lay on the doormat when he got back. He opened it immediately: bills didn't arrive in pink envelopes. The message was brief and filled him with apprehension.

Why are you ignoring me? Come round for tea this afternoon at five. My folks want to meet you. All my love, Camilla. PS. Why don't you get a phone?

The new home of Air Commodore Ralph Boyd, DFC, was a sight which Fred had managed to avoid during his short, passionate affair with the airman's daughter. It stood, he knew because Camilla had told him, in lofty isolation outside the town, surrounded by a paddock, a medieval longhouse (whatever that was) and two acres of professionally kept garden. Half a dozen undernourished serfs cowered, no doubt, in the outhouses.

It was the type of visiting that Fred had always strenuously avoided, feigning illness, previous appointments, deaths in the family and even, once, a car crash, but he couldn't see a way out of this.

He decided to cut out his second daily visit to bed and try to stay awake during the dreadful afternoon sleepiness that followed mid-day drinking. He was beginning to find that afternoon-mares were being added to the now normal night-mares that ended each day. He had a bath instead, found a clean blue shirt to go with the same old jeans and began to feel better. He sat down at his writing-desk and read the invitation again. There were two snags.

Fred's natural coolness towards top people in the forces (a coolness which he knew would be fervently reciprocated when the old buffer got the measure of the man who had laid siege to his lovely daughter) was snag number one. Snag number two was his ambiguous status with Camilla herself. Staying faithful to his own instructions to keep away from her, to avoid the emotional turmoil that she would sooner or later provide for him, had worked very well. He thought about her hourly, but with four miles between them she couldn't hurt him. Now he could see the problem. The note in the pink envelope proved it. The more aloof he became, the greater her interest was going to grow. Modern girls despised devotion; they needed the scent of the hunt.

All this was clear, and so when he left the flat at half past four he felt like a man who had been unknowingly programmed by some mind-bending department of the secret service.

Camilla wanted him.

As he walked up the lane which led to the Boyd residence she was waiting, smiling, on the huge swing gate.

"I thought you mightn't come," she said, kissing his cheek.

"You have only to snap your fingers."

Instead of snapping them, she wove them round his and led him cheerfully up the drive to the big house. She was wearing a dress today, white with blue flowers, that was high at the top and high at the bottom as well. Her legs were stocky but kissable.

"They're round the back on the patio," she said. "Don't be deceived by their manner, they're **very** interested in meeting you."

"I'm not sure this is a good idea," Fred replied, but they were already half way round the building and the Air Commodore's voice came round the corner at them, like a Lewis gun.

"... a rich bloody Yugoslav with a holiday home on the Adriatic. An antithesis of the Communist ethic, I'd have thought." The boom-boom-boom threatened to tell Yugoslavia to stand to attention.

The patio itself overlooked a rural valley with just a few very expensive houses on its far slopes. At the top, more than half a mile away, cows grazed in a field.

At the centre of the patio was a white wrought-iron table with four seats pulled up to it. At one of them, reading—and reading aloud from—a newspaper, was Camilla's father, a big man with white hair who was wearing a dark blue blazer with wings on the chest pocket, silver grey slacks and a white open-neck shirt. Next to him, behind some dark glasses, was an equally large woman, wearing trousers and an orange shirt-type blouse. Both looked up as Camilla and Fred appeared.

"Hello," shouted Mrs Boyd, and Fred imagined nervous sparrows abandoning trees a mile away. When Camilla had introduced him, they took the two empty chairs. Mrs Boyd dispensed Twining's Lapsang Souchong tea, and a plate of strawberries and cream.

Fred ate, drank, and waited. The Air Commodore discussed the merits of Communists owning holiday homes until the succulence of the strawberries distracted him. Then he told them about the barbecued antelope and fried termites he had once eaten in Africa. Mrs Boyd, behind her dark glasses, kept both eyes on Fred.

The Air Commodore's story about fried termites ended with a joke that only he appreciated.

"You're laughing for all of us, Ralph," said Mrs Boyd reprovingly.

"Laugh? I nearly bought my own gin," he said, chuckling.

He turned to his guest. "I don't remember Cam telling us. What do you do, Fred?"

Fred had many replies to this question. "I travel in ladies' underwear," had once produced an enlightening discussion on transvestism in the Cellar.

"Fred's a poet," said Camilla, before he could select an appropriate reply. He had rather fancied giving "prison governor" another airing; there were unused possibilities there.

"He writes poetry," Camilla added, as if the noun on its own would only confuse.

"What sort of poetry?" asked Mrs Boyd suspiciously. Her mind's list of desirable son-in-laws was extensive and surprisingly imaginative, but penniless poet wasn't on it.

"Bad poetry, mostly," Fred told her. "I'm writing one at the moment called Coffins Are Comfortable. It's about inflation."

He smiled at the Air Commodore, who began to look like a man who is being surreptitiously shat on by a malign pigeon in the rafters, but is too polite to draw attention to it.

"Have you sold any?" asked Mrs Boyd.

Fred shook his head.

"Well, Van Gogh never sold a painting."

Fred smiled across at the progeny of this privileged pair. She seemed apart from them, placed here by accident. The Air Commodore and his lady wife had not got the respectable, horse-riding, tennis-playing young lady that they undoubtedly wanted, but it was difficult to tell whether they knew. Their only child had come from another planet. She was young, wild, thoughtless, oversexed, irresponsible. He studied her tanned face and her green eyes and thought: a girl you'd give up smoking for.

Mrs Boyd was wrestling with an idea. "If you haven't sold any poetry," she said eventually, "what do you do for a living? I mean, what's your job?"

"I haven't got a job, Mrs Boyd," he said amiably.

It was a bit like somebody shouting Heil Hitler! in the middle of the two minutes' silence on Remembrance Sunday. The Air Commodore's head jerked like a puppet's.

"Why's that?" he asked crisply.

Fred stalled. "Several reasons."

The Air Commodore shook his head. "In my experience," he said, "there is only one reason why people do or don't do something. They think of others afterwards to justify themselves."

Fred thought: That's true. This chap wants watching. He said: "They always talk about people wanting jobs. People don't want jobs. They need money."

"I understand the one leads to the other," said the Air Commodore over his tea cup.

"Only in absurdly small quantities," said Fred mildly.

He decided that if he handled it properly he would manage to convey that, so far from being idle and out of work, he was in reality overwhelmingly ambitious and in no danger whatsoever of being fobbed off with anything trivial as a wage packet.

Mrs Boyd said, with surprising sympathy: "The unemployment is awful."

"Join the Air Force, Fred," said her husband. "I don't regret a minute of it."

Fred wanted to tell him, as politely as one could pass on such information, that he would sooner suck two pints of squitters through a used sock than spend a single day in uniform. Instead, he said: "I doubt whether I'd be an Air Commodore. It would all look rather different from the airmen's mess."

"Takes time," said Camilla's father, laughing. He opened the newspaper that had been resting on his lap. "What's on the television this evening, I wonder? Ninety minutes of baffling filth, I suppose. Probably a play about a half-caste homosexual prostitute."

"And his tortured relationship with a psychotic ponce," suggested Mrs Boyd gloomily.

Fred laughed loudly and realised with a shock that he rather liked Camilla's parents.

"Sex, sex, sex," said the Air Commodore. "You steer clear of it, Fred."

"He does," said Camilla.

Mrs Boyd looked at them both quickly and then reached for the teapot.

"More tea, anyone?" she asked.

Fred handed her his cup and then settled back to enjoy the view from the patio. But he found that when the conversation stopped, the thought of Oliver Oswald kept intruding.

Five

> Man is the only animal that laughs and weeps; for he is the only animal that is struck by the difference between what things are and what they might have been.
>
> **Hazlitt**

Like a Dominican monk of fifty, who still wonders whether he has a vocation, Fred lay in bed and considered Life. If the first minute of the day was the worst minute of the day there was something fundamentally wrong with one's life, but the view in every direction was now so cloudy that it was difficult to know where the repairs should begin.

He fancied a cigarette, but there was no ashtray in the bedroom—his only concession to the cancer scare. He reached out an arm and flicked on the transistor radio at his bedside. "... the firebrand Presbyterian pastor, a bastion of hardline Protestant policy for two decades ..." He switched it off quickly. Love, God isn't.

Eventually he felt able to get up, to resume, as he saw it, his acting, unpaid membership of the human race. One of these days, he knew for sure, the inside of his head would collapse and clouds of dust would billow from each ear.

A spider the size of a golf ball had commandeered the bath. Phobic about spiders, Fred decided to settle for a wash—bathing only destroyed the natural microbial flora, he told himself. Over the washbasin a battery of cosmetics stood in single file, a silent army that fought an endless battle to make him fit to mix with: a stick deodorant ("with the modern masculine fragrance"), a cologne, two varieties of after-shave, a spray-on foot deodorant ("avoid getting into eyes"), a breath purifier. This pricey collection had sent him out into the world on many occasions as an eminently suitable male lead in a seduction scene, or even sixth man at an orgy, but although he normally returned home celibate and angry his loyalty to the bottles did not diminish: he was now addicted to the smells.

In the kitchen he took three cod-liver-oil capsules, each containing no fewer than 4500 units of Vitamin A and 450 units of Vitamin D, all in one golden ball. It was a daily dosage he had lately augmented by Vitamin C, which played an important part in the formation of healthy blood, bones and teeth and in the healing of wounds. None of these good works was of the slightest interest to Fred, whose loyalty to the capsules was due entirely to the fact that since he started taking them, three years ago, he had never had a cold. Fred had preached the virtues of cod-liver capsules to anybody who would listen, but most people dismissed him as a hypochondriac as they sneezed in his face. He had recently considered buying a new tablet, Ginseng, the mysterious qualities of which could only be truly tested with the co-operation of a lady. Perhaps it was what he needed. Dear Sir, Before taking your tablet I could bend it with one hand. Now I can't bend it with two hands. Tell me, am I getting weaker or stronger?

Breakfast was always a problem. It would be so

easy to undo the good work of the pills. Butter was bad for you and so was milk. Eggs, tea, coffee and sugar were bad for you. It was difficult to find what was safe these days. Cheese was harmful, and so were chocolate, sweets, saccharine, meats, potatoes, artificial colourants, fried foods, charcoal grilled foods, infra-red cooked foods. Tuna fish was a health hazard and Döner kebabs were to be avoided. The list of dangers grew daily, if you believed what you read, and it wasn't confined to food: asbestos, the Pill, sex. Too much exercise was visibly harmful which was why all the top sportsmen in Britain looked at least ten years older than they were, but if you stayed in bed it was fatal.

Fred took the brave course and boiled an egg. While it rattled, split and leaked in the saucepan, he fetched the morning paper from the mat. The newsagent, with customary efficiency, had sent the wrong one, and he found himself gazing at a pictureless expanse of type and a front-page headline which read: Ireland—Is The Diaspora Over? (Fred's tastes in newspapers were more exoteric; they went for the "Vicar's Wife in Gang-Bang Horror" type of heading.) Beneath the headline was a graph showing the rising cost of Ireland to the British taxpayer. If this paper had covered the crucifixion, Fred thought, it would have had a graph on the front page showing the rising cost of timber. As an experiment, he had once read his daily newspaper one week late, every day for a month; it had helped him to appreciate the unimportance of most of its news.

The letter-box banged and he went out to find two letters on the mat. One had arrived in a long and shiny brown envelope that never meant good news; the other was in a larger than usual white envelope that obviously contained a card. The first message was an ungentle reminder that the bank, to its chagrin, was now banking with him. His attention was respectfully drawn to a twenty-pound overdraft.

He screwed the letter up and dropped it in his pedal bin. Let the debts zoom moonwards, he thought. That's what banks were for.

The second envelope carried an invitation to the wedding of Antony Brock and Wendy Scott. RSVP.

He made some toast and a pot of tea, retrieved the leaking egg, and set the whole lot up on the table in the kitchen. The wedding invitation reminded him of when he had combed the streets for a bride. Two or three years earlier he had thrown himself into the hunt with a determination that verged on panic. He wandered into shops, bars and restaurants, searching the premises in case the bewitching creature he sought was in there waiting. He never bothered to disguise his purpose.

"Can I help you, squire?" asked the barman in a pub in London.

"I'm looking for my wife," Fred told him.

"What does she look like?" asked the barman.

"I don't know," said Fred. "I haven't found her yet."

He was encouraged in his venture by Dermot, who was feeling much married and had decided that Fred should join him: the drowning man pulls down those nearest. Fred, he felt, wasn't putting enough energy into the business of finding a wife.

"You've got to get stuck in, Frederick, or you'll be reduced to sniffing bicycle saddles," he told him. "It's no good burying your head in the sand like an ostrich."

"Contrary to what you may think, Trader, ostriches don't bury their heads in the sand to hide from the world, but to hear the sound of approaching hooves. They want to know what's coming."

"Well, you're not coming. That's for sure."

"I will be, though, I will be. Once I find out where the hell the clitoris is, I'll be away."

And he was. During one dazzling summer he entertained an astonishing collection of girls in his flat. They stumbled into the street afterwards, a beatific smile on their faces, the sperm trickling down their thighs, and Fred developed a reputation—**homme fatal.** The younger and less experienced a woman was the more she excited him. The older women, with their veneer of experience, had a look in their eyes which shrivelled him. Young girls giggled, but not after they had lost their virginity. He seemed to spend half his life in bed and the other half in the bath. He drank milk, he ate steaks, he bought lettuce.

The orgy ended suddenly. He began to be haunted by an ineluctable truth: the total response that he was looking for in himself, instead of merely a genital one, never arrived. He was accepting too much second-rate sex. He became tired of entering into commitments when he was drunk that he would renege on when he was sober—declaring love in the early hours of the morning to girls who would repel him at dawn. His heart was in neutral. There had to be more to life than climbing on and off naked girls—not a lot more, but a bit more.

One day at the Saturday morning street-market that rcminded the town of its history, he thought that he had found what he was looking for in a girl called Melanie. She was a short dark-haired girl in a corduroy cap, a blue jump-suit with zip pockets, and cowboy boots. The whole ensemble was marginally less elegant than a volleyball player's knee-pads, and she talked too much about nothing in particular, but to Fred she was magic. Their friendship blossomed but remained determinedly platonic. Polite but firm rebuffs greeted his intermittent attempts to move it to the bedroom. By neither word nor action did Melanie reveal whether she knew how the human race had been reproducing itself all these years. She was his mate, but not his bedmate.

"If our relationship continues to develop like this, you could be best man at my wedding," he told her.

"That would be nice," she said.

He was baffled, but nothing could slake his lust,

not her taste in clothes, not her garrulous mediocrity, not even her mental infibulation. For him she shone.

The Melanie affair, ending in discord, slowed him down a little and he began to lose his impetus.

"Broken down by age and sex, as the statisticians say," Dermot told him.

He adopted the mien of the misogynist, eagerly copying out the verbal bullets of the sex war and sticking them to his kitchen wall. It didn't matter which side had fired them—the conflict was all:

Men's Lib: Educating a pretty girl is like pouring honey into a Swiss watch.
Women's Lib: A woman needs a man like a fish needs a bicycle.
Men's Lib: When she hands you a dishcloth, blow your nose on it, thank her, and hand it back.
Singles' Lib: Every married couple in the world, believing themselves uniquely jinxed, erects a bright facade around the slum of their private hell.

The messages were torn down and ritually burned the day after he met Camilla.

Fred phoned Ant. They had been close friends once, at school and afterwards, but their paths had diverged as Ant slipped from teenage to middle-age without any intervening period of riotous irresponsibility. Now he was sending out wedding invitations to his old friends.

Fred was curious. He wanted to know how the other half lived.

Ant, it transpired, had bought himself a £20,000 house in a quiet residential road not far from the station. It stood on its own in half an acre of ground with two huge trees in the front garden and a lawn sweeping away at the back to a large vegetable garden. Fred studied all this in some surprise before ringing the multi-chime doorbell.

Ant was short, stocky, smart. He wore a three-piece brown suit, Town Trek shoes, a wide-striped shirt with a silk tie. His face, beneath a mop of curly hair, was white and shiny and there were dark rings around the eyes.

"Come in, Fred," he said. "We'll crack a bottle of wine."

Fred followed him into the house. "How long have you had this?" he asked. "Did you win on the Premium Bonds?"

Ant showed him into the front room where a huge L-shaped settee faced a colour television in the opposite corner.

"I bought it last year," he said. "On a mortgage, of course. I took the deposit out of my piggy bank."

Ant was involved in some arcane activity to do with the commodity market. He spent many of his working hours talking about upside potentials, downside risks, gearing and leverage. Fred realised with a shock that he was already rich.

"I always thought that saving money was a fool's game," he said.

"Same old Fred," said Ant, wrestling with a corkscrew. "It's true that for some people inflation has made saving pointless. It is also true that if you'd been born on the same day as Jesus Christ and had saved a pound every day since you still wouldn't be a millionaire. However, I save more than a pound a day. And now I own a house."

He handed Fred a glass of wine, and sat in an armchair opposite him.

"What do you do all day?" said Fred. "I mean, what's your job about?"

"It's very interesting, actually. Tomorrow, for instance, I'm going on a course on zero base budgeting."

"Book now to ensure disappointment," said Fred. "I don't know how you do it."

Ant considered this in silence. In the old days, with

his deeply thoughtful expression, he had always been able to monopolise a conversation with his pauses.

"The human animal has to be kept working, Fred. It isn't geared for leisure."

"This human animal is," said Fred, sipping his wine. "Fifty weeks in the office and two weeks in Cleethorpes doesn't strike me as a very good deal."

"What are you doing?"

"I'm on skid row."

"Well," said Ant, "it doesn't seem to be making you very happy."

Fred shook his head. "I'm not going to win any prizes for bliss, Ant."

"An element of litotes, I think?"

Fred remembered Ant as the bright boy at school: he had a brain like razor blades. He was the wave of the future then, and now the future was here.

It occurred to Fred that his interest in his friends was far greater than their interest in him. Was this a strength or a weakness?

"Who is Wendy?" he asked. "This wedding invitation arrived today."

"Wendy is a nurse. Tall, slim, blonde."

"I remember her. The one with the finely drawn features and the wallet, as we used to say."

"That's her. We were wrong, though. I now have more money than her father. A great shame, but you can't have everything. Wendy is on duty, but she'll be in soon."

"She lives here?"

"Oh, yes."

Fred handed his empty glass across for a refill.

"What on earth do you want to marry her for, then?" he asked.

"It's what people do, Fred."

"It's not what I do. It's unhealthy. The kids bring germs home from school giving you one cold after another. You'll get ringworm off the cat, hard-pad off the dog, soft chancres off the maid. I've heard about this domestic life, Ant. It's bloody dangerous."

He couldn't resist the urge to make fun of this man, but Ant was much too serious these days for Fred's brand of humour: the years had rolled on, the perspectives had altered. He now regarded Fred as a frivolous person—he had been seen once coming out of a bar.

Through the window, Fred saw a saloon car glide into the drive. It was a very expensive model.

"What about all the girls you'll never be able to have?" he asked. There must be something he could say that would jolt his conventional old friend.

"I could never get girls, anyway," said Ant. "They thought I was too serious, too humourless, too money-oriented."

"They did?"

A key scratched in the front door and Wendy came in.

"Hallo, dear," said Ant, standing up.

Fred stood up, too. He was watching a staid married couple.

"This is Fred, an old friend of mine," said Ant.

Wendy looked at him warily. "I've seen you before," she said.

"Rolling round the streets, vomiting into waste-paper baskets?"

"Probably," said Wendy. "Give me a wine, dear."

Ant did so quickly. He was clearly in love—or what passed for love in this part of the world—but when Wendy turned to listen to him, Fred was sure that it wasn't reciprocated. She didn't look at him in the way that he looked at her. He was sure, too, that his encroachment upon this cosy domestic scene was deeply resented by the future Mrs Brock. She had got what she wanted and it didn't include Fred. Ant had got what he wanted, too: a respectable wife. And he would never know the financial agonies that most people were concealing.

Fred moved towards the door, depressed. "I must go to see my broker," he said. "My pawnbroker."

Ant didn't smile. "Cheer up, Fred," he said. "Life isn't as worrying as you think. If you were about to die, you'd realise that."

On Thursday evenings Fred and Dermot played darts for one of the town's pubs. There were five pairs in each team and Fred and Dermot always threw last in the hope that the match would be tied when they went to the board and hero status awaited them.

They sat in the corner of a crowded public bar and waited for their turn to throw. Dermot fixed the plastic flights to his tiny tungsten alloy darts and laid them on the table in front of him. Fred took whatever darts were available; he played an unpredictable game.

A big man in a blue nylon shirt that flapped over his trousers threw his darts with surprising finesse. Each thud against the board was followed by delighted shouts from his team. The scorer with the chalk was a wizard of mental arithmetic.

Dermot gazed round the smoky room.

"When you look at a map of the world and think about all those sun-drenched places where you can survive on a few pounds a week, you can't help wondering why you have chosen this spot to settle," he said.

"Well, why did you?"

"I got married young. My wife likes it here. She doesn't trust abroad. But I was thinking about you—you're single. It's a different world altogether when you're woken by the sun instead of an alarm clock. Down the beach for a dip before breakfast. It amazes me that people settle for so much less than they could have. They behave as if they're going to live for three hundred years." He picked up the cyder that he always drank on darts nights and sipped it thoughtfully. "You know what Adam Smith said about the workers? What pissed him off about them was the poverty of their aspirations. It applies to us all."

"I doubt whether he said pisses off," said Fred. "He had a great respect for the language. Still, I'm the convert you're looking for. There's a simple truth about this world. It hit me the other day after the fourth pint: most people never expose themselves to the risk of anything interesting happening to them."

"It's too late for me. I've lost the sense of adventure. I enjoy the familiar—the unfamiliar disconcerts us oldsters. But you're ten years younger than me. You know all about everybody else wasting their lives, but what about you? You worry me to death, to tell you the truth."

Fred stared across at the noisy darts players: some people found happiness easily.

"I've got as much future as a toilet roll," he said. "Identical future, come to think of it. It's all very well saying that I could live cheaply on one of those sun-drenched beaches, but where does even the little money that I would need come from?"

"You could always sell sperm to the Americans," said Dermot. "They pay fifty pounds for a sample, I was reading yesterday. You could make seven hundred quid a week if you don't sprain your wrist."

"I don't fancy having 'wanker' on my passport. The one job I've always wanted, though, is sex investigator on one of those Sunday papers. 'She lowered her panties and smiled invitingly. I made an excuse and came.'"

"I made an excuse and left is what they usually write."

"Oh well, I wouldn't be any good at that then."

A roar greeted the conclusion of one of the games.

"We're losing two-one," said Dermot. "We may be called upon to save the day."

A young bank clerk who seemed to flick the darts out of his right ear went to the board to practise for the fourth game. His partner, a small blond man who earned seven times as much money as he did by crawling up eighteen-inch gas pipes under the streets of southern England, stood square to the board and seemed to launch the darts from his nose.

The team captain, a permanently unemployed young man called Danny, came over.

"You two are quiet tonight," he said cheerfully. "Wrong time of the month, is it?"

"How would you like a mouthful of signet rings?" said Dermot.

Fred went to the bar to buy some drinks before their game. The barmaid was telling a friend about her boyfriend, Max. Fred concluded, from the way that she spoke, that this was either her first romance or her last. He took the drinks back to Dermot.

The man who crawled up gas pipes had tied the match by going out on 156. Even his opponents applauded.

Fred went to the board and found some darts. They were longer than average, and heavier. Aiming for twenty, he hit one. Aiming for nineteen, he hit three.

"It's up to you two," said Danny. "Pints if you win."

Fred improved, but Dermot excelled. They won in two straight games.

Danny bought them pints.

"How do you survive without working, Danny?" Fred asked him.

"I get unemployment money, don't I?"

"Unemployment money? I hadn't thought of that."

"You don't even have to collect it. They post it to you."

"Welcome to the welfare state."

Dermot came over.

"Must go. I have a date with my wife."

"She's waiting for you, is she?"

"She is. Eagerly. I told her, if I'm not there start

without me. Something is happening tomorrow evening, but I can't remember what it is."

"They're choosing the carnival queen."

"Ah yes. Camilla. Have you seen her lately?"

"She dropped in this afternoon."

"I don't think you want me," she had said as they lay naked on his bed. His lack of enthusiasm wasn't something that she could miss.

The curtains were drawn against the bright July sun and there seemed to be something deliciously decadent about a mid-afternoon rendezvous, with Camilla sprawled across his bed, while the world outside rolled up its sleeves and worked. But how could he explain his failure to react?

"Have you found somebody else?"

"Obviously, no."

"I don't see what's obvious about it."

She leaned over towards him, pressing her breasts against his face.

"Don't you fancy me any more?"

For a moment Fred thought that it was going to work—a hint of a movement, floodgates opening—but the moment passed.

"Rigid, it ain't," she said.

Mental illness, physical illness, impotence, thought Fred. I'm ripe for religion.

She ran her hand up and down his thigh, just missing the area of inactivity.

"What's the matter, pudding?" she asked. "How can your body possibly reject my body?"

"Perhaps I'm past it. A lot of people have died, you know, by the time they reached my age. According to the gerontologists, the longest active life-span goes to intelligent, optimistic, happily married aristocrats. That gives me a life expectancy of about two minutes."

"Ganda women excite their husbands by tickling their armpits," she said.

"Not quite what I need."

"What is the matter? You've been strange since you came home. Is something worrying you?" She pulled herself back and looked at him.

Is something worrying me? he thought. Surely not. I have very little money left and further supplies of it are going to be harder to find than a foreskin in a synagogue. I lack the qualifications for work that might interest me, and seem to have become psychologically incapable of work that doesn't. I have committed the supreme folly of losing you in a game of poker, and the egregious Mr Oswald is about to make my life intolerable if I don't persuade you to sleep with him. The past is painful, the present purgatory, and the future, which extends no further than tomorrow, is problematical, and nothing less than a frontal lobotomy is going to cope with my boundless pessimism. I lack faith and hope, and charity is beyond my resources. I can't get a job, I can't even get an erection, and, as a cosy, all-embracing bonus, one of the most distinguished psychiatrists in Britain is convinced that I shouldn't even be allowed out.

He said: "I'm fine."

"Parts of you aren't."

"Appetite comes with eating, as Rabelais said. Only he said it in French."

"Do you want me to eat you?"

"I meant that the sexual appetite is very like the appetite for food. The more you have, the more you want. You work your way up to six women or twelve meals a day. On the other hand, if you eat very little your stomach shrinks to the size of a walnut and soon you want very little."

"It's not your stomach that has shrunk."

"Metaphorically it is."

But he knew it wasn't true. It wasn't the sexless life that he had led for three months that had curbed his desire. It was the abortion that had emasculated him. The ram was now a gelding. Cardboard Fred, clit-teaser. His mind turned to dildos, douche nozzles, beer bottles, vibrators, cucumbers, water sprays—the world was full of Fred-substitutes. He was even redundant in the bedroom.

Not quite remembering why, he left the flat early the following morning and headed for a single-storey, grey-brick building just a hundred yards along the road. At one time it had been called the Labour Exchange, and afterwards it became the Department of Employment. Today its title was the Employment Office, but by next week Britain's busy civil servants would no doubt have dreamed up a new name to pin up over its dreary door.

Inside sad youngsters scanned green walls covered with postcards; each card bore the details of a job. Unemployment might be on its way to two million but here, if you could find it, was work. A hotel required staff, Fred noticed. A busy workshop would like to meet a skilled cellulose sprayer.

He walked past the cards and went into the office.

"I'd like to register as unemployed," he told a young clerk who was thumbing his way through a card index system.

"Go into that room over there and see Mr Ringrose," said the clerk without looking up.

Mr Ringrose, thick-rimmed spectacles and a small black moustache, looked harassed, as if finding fresh jobs for the unemployed hordes was no longer compatible with keeping one's sanity. He sat at a large, almost empty desk, with a telephone at each elbow. A poster on the wall behind his head asked: Are You About To Be Made Redundant?

"Sit down," he said. "Name?" The dark green walls, standard decor throughout the building, reminded Fred of the classroom.

"How many O-levels have you got, Mr Carton?" he asked.

"Eleven."

"Eleven? Good Christ—and you can't get a job? The world's in a mess. I tell you, the world's in a mess."

Fred nodded. The world was in a mess.

"I want a carpenter, a bricklayer, a mechanic, a plumber, a painter and a gardener," said Mr Ringrose, without consulting any notes. "Also a part-time school-cleaner. Not your sort of thing at all, I suppose?" He pulled a sheet of paper from a drawer in his desk and mumbled to himself: "Hairdresser, insurance agent, butcher, shop assistant, chef."

Fred watched him and decided, for future reference, that a man could wear glasses or grow a moustache, but not both. The human face wasn't large enough to carry so much furniture.

"Can you drive, Mr. Carton?"

"I've a licence, but no car."

"Can you type?"

"No."

"Could you sell things? Have you got the gift of the gab?"

Familiar waves of depression broke over Fred and he stood up quickly. This had been a mistake.

Mr Ringrose, not noticing, talked on. "We've cocked it up, you see. We educate our youngsters too well. Their expectations can't be met. Eleven O-levels! What I want is four labourers out at the sewage works. No wonder the immigrant workers are flooding into northern Europe. Our own kids are trained for marvellous jobs that don't exist. Have you seen the art school? Hundreds of brilliant young artists coming off the conveyor belt every year! Who on earth let them get on it? Artists? Who needs them?"

Fred walked slowly to the door. He suddenly felt sick. "This place depresses me," he said.

"You can register for unemployment benefit," said Mr Ringrose. "After three weeks, you'll get . . ."

Fred shook his head.

"I don't want to join," he said.

The County Country Club stood in its own splendid grounds just over a mile from the town centre. It had once been the luxury home of a minor peer who had servants and horses to prove it, but succeeding government measures had impoverished his descendants and they sold the building to a brewery, who knocked four rooms into a dining-hall and dance-floor, and two more into an olde worlde bar. It was now the haunt of many retired colonels, who lived in the rural areas converting their pensions into gin, and most of the district's richer businessmen, who found that the flexibility of a bar's drinking hours increased in direct proportion to its distance from the nearest police station. It was also much used for social functions, charity dances, masonic dinners and fashion shows.

Fred arrived with an Arab sheikh at nine o'clock. The Arab sheikh was Trader Ryan, who had bought the clothes in a job lot that afternoon and decided that they suited him.

The dance-floor was crowded with a hundred couples, and beyond them a band of half a dozen middle-aged musicians was doing something painful to a tune that had made a memorably brief incursion into the hit parade some eight years before. The dance which launched the carnival and town show was for charity, and all the best people were in the club, striving to be noticed.

"I think I've got syphilis of the arm-pit," said Dermot loudly, scratching himself. "Funny—I don't remember giving anyone a Bombay shuffle lately."

He looked round, but the noise of the band denied him the shock effect that he had intended.

"Behave yourself," said Fred, "or I won't bring you out to these posh places." Neither would have been within hearing distance of tonight's racket, he reflected, if Camilla had not been winning a hundred pounds from Oliver Oswald by competing for the title of carnival queen.

"I make people laugh, kiddo, and that's better than making them growl. Lead me to the alcoholic nourishment."

They bought large gins and found a table at the edge of the dance-floor. Couples gliding past eyed Trader curiously. You didn't get a lot of foreigners around here.

For half an hour there was no sign of either judges or carnival queen entrants, but then the band stopped and a chatty little man in a pale blue jacket came to the front of the stage, adjusted the microphone to his own lack of height, and called for silence. His request was granted, but only slowly.

They were, he announced proudly, about to select the town's carnival queen and two attendants from the twelve finalists who had been chosen earlier, but first he would like to introduce the four judges. The judges were all very important people right up to the town border and nonentities beyond: the chairman of the council, a greengrocer called Brent who was so startlingly illiterate that he had been on the council for twenty-four years before his colleagues had finally succumbed to his claim for the top office; the chairman of the Town Show and Carnival Committee, a man betrayed into an early marriage by a powerful lust, the father of a teenage son at thirty-two and now, heredity being what it is, a somewhat surprised grandfather at thirty-eight; a neurotic and angular woman who seemed to get involved in most of the approved activities in the town purely because of her tendency to arrange flowers where more than six people had gathered together; and "Councillor Oliver Oswald, chairman of the Open Spaces Committee."

"The open spaces are between his ears," Dermot told a woman at the next table, but she looked away. He leaned across, confidentially, to Fred. "Ryan's quips are going down like a cup of cold sick tonight, Frederick."

The four judges, applauded with what Fred regarded as a hopelessly inappropriate respect, took seats at a long table on one side of the stage, and the man in the pale blue jacket revealed that he was going to interview each contestant first, and then they would all appear on stage together before the judges made their decision. Encountering no opposition to this plan, he called into the microphone: "Number one, Camilla Boyd," rather like a man who has unexpectedly produced Bob Hope to top the bill at the village hall.

Considerable applause, bolstered strongly by the male half of the guests, greeted the arrival on stage of a deeply sun-tanned Camilla in a short white dress that plunged pleasantly at the front.

Dermot muttered: "The rest haven't got a prayer. One-horse race, as my old granny used to say."

Fred sipped his gin and watched Camilla. The reluctant entrant blossomed at the mike. Blue jacket asked her a predictable question about what changes she would like to see in this lovely old town, and she spoke forcefully about the need for a community centre where young people could meet in the evenings for film shows, music or drama, and went on to ask why this town, alone of any for miles, had no squash courts.

Blue jacket, abashed, said: "What an interesting conversation."

"It's all right for you," said Camilla. "You've got me to talk to."

She left the stage to long applause that doomed what followed to anti-climax.

Like most bachelors, Fred revived in the company of beautiful women, and he sat back to study the competition. Most of the contestants' faces were familiar, and Dermot was able to provide background information that was evidently not available to the man in the blue jacket.

"That one goes like a fiddler's elbow," he said when a tall redhead replaced Camilla at the microphone. The next competitor, shorter and stockier with brown hair swept up at the back, was, apparently, so boring that even men making obscene phone calls hung up. A willowy ash blonde waltzed on to launch a promising attack on the smugness and complacency of the town and its inhabitants before one of her contact lenses vanished under an eyelid and she lost her drift.

"I'm not going to find anything here tonight," said Dermot.

"Don't be so fussy," said Fred. "One of those girls would love to get laid by a sheikh."

Dermot snorted. "You can always stoop and pick up nothing, as my old granny used to say."

"Your old granny sounds a bit of a drag to me."

"She'd have come second tonight, kiddo."

On stage, the interviews were over and all the girls filed back into view for a final appearance before the judging.

"Here they are!" shouted blue jacket. "Camilla, Evelyn, Jill, Janice, Judith, Terry, Christine, Angela, Lynn, Carol, Susan and Linda." The applause rose and fell from different corners of the room, and the girls left the stage while the judges conferred. Fred watched Oliver Oswald, public figure tonight in smart brown suit and dark green shirt, controlling a whispered discussion that didn't last very long. The band played "Diamonds Are a Girl's Best Friend."

Five minutes later, blue coat was back in action calling out the third placed girl first and then the second. The winner—the unanimous winner—was Camilla Boyd, who appeared solemnly to a musical fanfare and was crowned by Greengrocer Brent.

As the girls came down the steps from the stage, Dermot was on his feet to grab one of the losers.

"How about you and me blowing our minds on a

half of Guinness?" he asked. The girl that he cornered had a small, round face that her short life had already moulded into a compliant smile. She nodded.

Fred went off to stock up on gin and was intercepted by Oliver Oswald.

"Evening, Fred," he said.

"I see you've lost a hundred pounds," Fred replied. "Drink?"

Oliver shook his head and placed a hand on his shoulder.

"I'm glad you mentioned betting debts," he said. "When do you deliver?"

Over his shoulder Fred could see the new carnival queen dancing with Greengrocer Brent. The event was being recorded by a photographer from the local newspaper.

"Deliver?" said Fred.

"You know what I'm talking about. There's some unfinished business between us."

Out of the bar and placed in this new environment, there was an edge to Oliver Oswald that he had not seen before. His hand slipped off Fred's shoulder and reappeared in front of his face, index finger pointing. For a moment, forgetting the man was a councillor, he thought that Oliver was going to hit him.

"I owe Camilla a hundred pounds for taking part in this business tonight. If you're not paying your debts, I'm not paying mine. She won't get a penny. Until. I think it should be you who explains that to her."

He was gone in the crowd, his face angry and white, and was replaced almost immediately by Dermot.

"She won't dance," he said sadly, "and if she won't dance she won't go to bed. That's rule 23a."

"What's rule 23b?"

"If she won't go to bed, I won't dance. Rule 23 covers dancing."

Camilla came up.

"Hello, pudding. Kiss the queen."

He kissed her nose. "Did you enjoy yourself out there?"

There was a crowd around them now, staring at Camilla. Fred, embarrassed at the attention, eased her away from them and towards the bar.

"I did not. That wasn't my sort of thing at all. But I made myself some money didn't I? Let's go and find Mr Oswald. I want my hundred pounds."

"He seems to have disappeared," said Fred.

Six

Life is a disease with mortality rate of
one hundred per cent.
Doctor Geoffrey Spencer

The following Friday evening police sealed off the town's streets to traffic. As they became empty, the pavements began to fill up with people, who were soon crowding five or six deep on both sides of the road. Children danced and waved balloons, threw streamers, blew whistles, all of which they had badgered their parents into buying from astute street traders who had moved in for the carnival. A new and cheerful atmosphere was created by the occasion: even the policemen were smiling.

Fred and Dermot had more important business, and they only appeared from the door of the Cellar with full pint mugs when they could hear the band in the distance. It was a small military band, produced from nowhere for the evening and, behind three men on white horses, it led the procession. Behind the band was a long, green lorry on which sat carnival queen Camilla, in mauve cape, and her two attendants in yellow. They sat round a pergola of roses and a fountain that appeared to be working. Over forty floats followed them: the scouts, the nurses, several schools, a car firm advertising a new luxury model, a factory with about twenty "cavemen" dancing on a lorry and squirting the crowd with water, a bank throwing away dummy pound notes, the local theatre, the Round Table, a lifeboat appeal, the Conservative Club, two pubs and many shops and businesses who were delighted at this opportunity to advertise their existence.

As the floats rolled by, girls threw fruit, chocolates and leaflets into the crowd.

"I don't approve of all this jollity," said Fred. "Why aren't these people working?"

The procession moved slowly, stopping occasionally and concertina-ing before moving off again and eventually leading the way up the wide Georgian street that brought them into the park at the top of the town. It was here that the carnival merged into a town show and fun fair that went on all weekend.

Fred and Dermot followed the crowds in the direction of the park. Somewhere among the thousands, Camilla was waiting to be rescued.

The park had been transformed into a city of marquees. They surrounded the main arena, where several spectaculars involving fearless motor-cyclists, windswept musicians, tug-of-war teams and well trained dogs were scheduled during the show. Greengrocer Brent, with some chain contraption round his neck, was declaring the show open as they arrived, and those people who had taken part in the procession were leaping off their floats.

"I said I'd meet the carnival queen in the bar," said Fred. "Which one of these tents is."

"Let us locate it."

They wandered through the evening crowds from marquee to marquee: one was filled with a display of flowers, another with cage birds and rabbits. In the wine-makers' tent there were hundreds of bottles of homemade hooch, looking like urine samples in a police laboratory, and, in another, one of the canine competitors in the dog obedience tests was disobediently mounting a rival who was obediently submitting.

"The judging's tomorrow," said Dermot. "Rabbits, cats, birds, dogs, flowers, vegetables, wines—where do they get all the judges from? If you stand around here long enough you're sure to get a highly commended label slapped on your forehead."

Between the police tent and the cystic fibrosis tent they found an exhibition put on by the council which, apart from boasting about its sterling work over drainage and street lighting, provided a history of the town, with models, diagrams, newspaper cuttings and photographs that were brown and faded at the edges. The pictures showed the town fifty, a hundred, two hundred years ago: few towns in the world could have changed so little. Soon they were both engrossed in the cuttings. On 15 March 1902 the local coroner had reported that nineteen out of twenty suicides removed their hats before killing themselves. A story printed on 9 October 1886 said: "A mechanic named Thomas Oates has just died from hydrophobia. The deceased was bitten by a cat about eighteen months ago and until a few weeks back there were no symptoms beyond a little indifference to his friends." Underneath this, they read:

> Francis Price forfeited his life on the gallows on Monday for the murder of his sweetheart Sarah Pratt on 18 April last. It may be remembered that the prisoner was of the same age as his victim (24) and had been paying his addresses to the deceased, who rejected his suit, and that as she refused to be reconciled and make it up he cut her throat with a shoemaker's knife which he had sharpened for that purpose. He was tried at the

Assizes on 4 August, found guilty on the clearest evidence and sentenced to death by Mr Justice Williams.

Since his condemnation he has, under the ministrations of the Rev. T. Collins (Wesleyan), manifested great penitence and contrition, constantly praying for the forgiveness of his sins, and saying that Sarah Pratt had "gone to glory". He frequently exhorted his fellow-prisoners to lead a better life; he also managed Bible classes and drew up for his minister the particulars of his career as a shoemaker, soldier, runaway apprentice and professional runner.

The extreme penalty of the law was carried into effect on Monday at ten o'clock. At that hour the executioner, who performed the same office on Palmer, came on the scaffold in front of the county gaol and placed the noose round Price's neck. The criminal, while on the brink of eternity, prayed fervently that God would forgive his sins.

The customary signal was given, the bolt withdrawn and after two or three convulsive movements, the murderer's body was left hanging motionless from the beam. There were about 1,500 persons present.

The hangman (George Smith) received some rather rough treatment before leaving the town. It appears that Price failed to give his signal by dropping his handkerchief and Smith, wishing to complete his work as soon as possible, withdrew the bolt without it. Hence the indignation of the crowd, some of whom violently assaulted him at the railway station. Mr Chiltern, the station-master, rescued him from the mob, and locked him in a second-class waiting-room until the next up-train. The fury of the people was meanwhile spent.

"Poor hangman," said Fred. "I wonder how many innocent people he killed during his career?"

Dermot looked thoughtful. "I've never understood capital punishment. Punish a man by cutting his hand off and they call it barbaric. Put a noose round his neck and hang him and they call it civilised. Ask the prisoner which he'd prefer! It takes six minutes to kill a man in the electric chair and the blood boils. Where's the alcohol?"

In the corner of the park was the eight-hundred-year-old manor house which had provided bed and breakfast for several kings and queens, but not lately. Historians pottered around it nowadays with thoughtful expressions on their faces, and tourists arrived regularly with cameras dangling on their chests. During the Civil War the house had been surrendered by the local Royalist commander to the Parliament forces. According to Dermot, this was the last exciting event to have taken place in the town.

The beer tent was next to a smaller tent that was promoting the evening classes now available to local adults with an unquenchable thirst for knowledge; esoteric information offered nightly in draughty halls ranged from Aztec mythology to origami.

A row of trestle tables running down one side of the beer tent was the bar counter, and among the crowd in front of it Councillor Oliver Oswald, chairman of the Open Spaces Committee, was being photographed with Miss Camilla Boyd, carnival queen. She looked very small beside him.

"I'm sick of seeing Oliver's picture in the paper," Dermot said. "When the flash goes off he always manages to look like someone who has been caught with his hand up the Guide mistress's knickers."

Fred was sick of seeing Oliver in the flesh. The man had become an obstacle to whatever peace of mind was going. He wanted him to go a long way away—on the other side of the asteroid belt would be quite near enough.

"I wonder what it costs to have someone wiped out?" he asked.

"About five thousand pounds," said Dermot. "It depends on the time-scale, whether the body has to be disposed of, that sort of thing. Why do you ask?"

"I don't want that man to irritate me any more."

"What is it about the lovely Oliver that irritates you exactly?"

"He's breathing."

Camilla was wearing a short red dress with a high waist. Her blonde hair, after a late afternoon visit to the hairdressers, had been partially gathered on the top of her head and fixed into a pony tail which covered her shoulders. She looked like an early photograph of Brigitte Bardot. Oliver Oswald was obviously hypnotised by her, and greeted Fred's arrival with a perceptible lack of enthusiasm. He continued with a joke he was telling.

"So the bloke at the window says: 'Never you mind yonder star. You get them bloody camels off my lawn.'"

Camilla laughed politely.

"Hello, pudding," she said. "I didn't see you from the float. Weren't you watching?"

"We certainly were. You looked stunning."

"We were just outside the Cellar," said Dermot.

"Of course you were," said Camilla.

"Good evening, you layabouts," said Oliver Oswald.

The temporary nature of the bar had restricted the choice of drink and they settled for large gins. It was strange drinking on grass.

Fred watched Oliver Oswald fussing round Camilla. It was a warm August evening and he was wearing a dark grey suit, His skin leaked sweat and he had grown, Fred noticed, a vicious hairline moustache. People were moving in on him, ostensibly to discuss the show. But with the carnival queen at his elbow, he had become, for once, attractive company.

"I must take the lady away from you for a few moments," he said. "I promised to introduce her to the show chairman. It's the only nice thing that is going to happen to him this weekend, poor bastard."

"I'll see you later," Camilla said.

Fred drank his gin and stared out of the tent at the crowds. He liked the town show because it was different and because of the fun fair which came with it; but the show's basic programme reinforced his doubts about the people around him. Who were these characters who stayed at home, made jam, poured it into jars and brought it to the park in the hope of being told that it was better than the jam that their neighbour had made? Who were these people who took their dogs to dog obedience classes once a week in the hope of winning a prize at the town show? And if people wanted to make gallons of wine at home, what a good idea—but why did they have to be so damn competitive about it?

"Hello, mate," said a voice at his shoulder. A very short man in built-up shoes and an immaculate suit with matching waistcoat was smiling up at him. Fred remembered the whey face, but not with pleasure. It had tinted, rimless glasses and lots of tight curls over the top. His name was Fortescue, and Fred remembered his hurrying around on busy little legs at school in a manner which ingratiated him with everyone except his fellow-pupils. Nothing is good enough for Fortescue, they used to say, and now he had it: he was number six in a bank.

"What are you doing, Fred?" he asked. "I've seen very little of you since leaving school."

And many doorways I've had to hide in, thought Fred. "Nothing. I'm out of work. Unemployable."

"Surely not," said Fortescue, but the satisfied glint in his eyes said, "it's no surprise to me."

Fortescue had the security of the bank round him. He smiled happily. There was no happiness like the happiness of a simple man.

"Just look at that beautiful lady over there," said Dermot. "The short black hair and the legs. Anyone know who she is?"

"She's my wife," said Fortescue.

"Is she really?"

"We're married. I'm her spouse."

"I don't believe you," said Fred, who had once taken the girl out.

"Man and wife," said Fortescue.

"What's her name then?" asked Dermot.

"Trade secret."

"Extraordinary name."

"She's Mrs Fortescue," said Fred. "I used to fancy her."

"So did I," said Fortescue sadly.

Fred recalled her marvellously quizzical expression, a strange tilting of the eyes which promised magical things if only you could be alone. It took him some days to discover that an expression was all she had and, occasionally, even that vanished.

"I must go to her," said Fortescue. "She's lonely." His little legs scampered over the grass.

"Poor old Fortescue," said Fred. "What will become of him?"

"He'll grow old, go grey and die," said Dermot. "It's quite common."

They watched the reunion of the Fortescues.

"I'm surprised he got her," said Fred. "What the hell does she see in a stupid little fart like that?"

Dermot shook his head. "Any man can get any woman he wants. I'm convinced of it. He only has to put up a big enough display of affection. It's his desire that decides it. The women are happy enough with their devoted husbands. Extraordinary, really."

Fred felt a deep and irrational hatred for the Fortescues of this world. How could they convince themselves that they had handled their lives so smartly? How could they look so damned pleased with themselves when they had achieved so little? It was as if they had somehow cheated in the quest for happiness, found a short cut through the pain.

At that moment the lights of the fair were

switched on and the raucous woodwind of fairground music filled the park. Fred and Dermot finished their drinks and went outside. Soon, huge wheels were turning against the darkening sky, roundabouts were hurtling, rifle shots were cracking in the background, absurdly light wooden balls were being thrown furiously at coconuts on sticks, and bumping cars were drawing delighted screams from dozens of youthful throats.

"I love fairs," said Dermot. "Where shall we start?"

They walked up to one end and watched people queueing for the ghost train. The people who were reappearing through the swing doors did not seem to be noticeably excited by what they had seen, and they moved on to the next attraction, which was an invitation to see a two-headed monster. They ignored both this and the haunted house, and spent a lot of money at a coconut shy, where they failed to dislodge a single coconut. At the next stall they each won a coconut throwing three darts into a playing card and at the stall after that they won two more by knocking five tins off a shelf with three balls. They gave all four coconuts to a small girl who had watched, enthralled, and, infected by the prevailing gaiety, headed for the big wheel. They were strapped in, side by side, and the wheel lurched upwards and then stopped while someone was strapped in below them. Then it began to turn, giving them a fine view of the fair and the show and, finally at the top, the whole town.

"That will be more than enough of that," said Fred, when they were safely down. "Let's find something a little more gentle."

The town's whole population seemed to be in the park now, packing the fair and giving it the correct carnival atmosphere. Darkness crept down and the fair's lights stood out in the night. Later the children would be taken home and the drunks would arrive and fights would break out behind the marquees, but by then Fred would have gone. He stopped at the noughts and crosses machine and played three draws with it while Dermot, who had decided against gentleness, hurled through the night on the octopus. Fred had received a faintly signalled message during his circuits on the big wheel that too much of that type of activity could very easily put the beer and gin that was presently inside him outside him.

He abandoned the noughts and crosses machine and looked round at the crowds. Where was the carnival queen? She had certain duties to perform, he knew. She had to pull the winning ticket out of a drum in a raffle for a car; she had to be photographed with Greengrocer Brent at the council's exhibition; she was even one of the judges in a contest to find the Young Artist of the Year. But these chores which came with her instant and ephemeral celebrity could not take more than an hour. Other more plausible explanations for her disappearance arrived slowly. Perhaps the Air Commodore had recently delivered a short lecture to his only daughter on the qualities and characteristics that one would hope to find in a son-in-law. Perhaps the only daughter herself had become disillusioned with his present inability to make love. His problem showed no sign of going away and it worried him so much now that he seldom thought about it. The Unit had taught his mind one thing, to avoid dangerous corners.

"How are your sexual impulses?" Doctor Jago had asked him during one of their sessions together. His bald head gleamed under the strip lighting.

"There's not a lot of opportunity in here to find out," Fred told him.

"There are certain physical consequences of a temporary nature to the sort of mental experience that you have had. It's not anything to worry about. I'm writing a book about it, as a matter of fact."

"I know," said Fred. He began to wonder whether

he might appear as a footnote. (The case of Frederick John Carton, quondam stud, is an interesting example of this syndrome. A young man who had previously enjoyed an above average amount of sexual experience, he suffered a mental collapse when his girlfriend elected to have an abortion rather than marry him. He subsequently found that intercourse was beyond his powers. He became morose, peevish, introspective, torpid . . .)

"The physical illness that is linked to the mental illness," said Doctor Jago, "and the mental illness that is linked to the physical illness."

It was at about this time that Fred decided that taking part in a serious conversation in the Unit was like wading thigh-deep through treacle.

But now the physical illness had arrived—and just at the moment when Camilla was chasing him. Or had she stopped all that? If she had already wandered off into the night, bored with their agamic existence, and decided to find a lover, she had certainly chosen the right evening. Today the whole town fancied her.

The beer tent was crowded but with years of experience behind him he had his hand round a large gin very quickly.

"There you are," whispered Camilla, appearing from nowhere. "I always know where to find you."

She looked excited and happy and he kissed her mouth.

"I thought I'd lost you," he said.

"Busy! I've been so busy! You'll have to buy the local paper next week. With all the pictures they've taken of me there won't be room for anything else."

"Have a drink."

"I'll get it," said Oliver Oswald.

Fred hadn't realised he was there.

"Oliver has invited us back to his place for a few drinks afterwards," said Camilla. "Isn't that nice of him?"

Not even Oliver Oswald knew what drinks he had offered to his guest, and by two o'clock they could hardly tell bacardi from whisky. Fred had drunk so much that it seemed to be forcing his eyes out of the front of his head. The three of them sat in deep armchairs, pulled up to one of the small onyx tables that was covered in bottles.

"Trixie has left me," said Oliver, waving a bottle of something.

"Left you?" said Fred, draining his glass.

"Walked out yesterday. Left me a note. Cheers!" He introduced the bottle to the glass but it was empty.

"What is she going to do for money?" Camilla asked.

"A woman's question," said Oliver. "No doubt her solicitor will be telling me about that. Anyway, I'm looking for a new wife. Get them to send in their applications. You know my tastes, anything in skirts."

Fred could imagine him marrying again very quickly. All his m[illegible] friends who had been involved in a divorce had remarried as soon as possible, but whether this was an unsolicited testimonial for the married state, or merely fresh corroboration of his friends' weakness with women, he was never sure.

"What did the note say?" he asked.

"'Good-bye, you fat slob,' I think. My wife isn't very literary."

"She doesn't sound very nice either," said Camilla doubtfully.

"I won't argue with that," said Oliver Oswald. "It was my mistake. Never propose when you've got an erection. That's my message to the world. I tell you, being undersexed is an asset these days. I only wish I were. Sometimes I think that my response to women is out of all proportion to what they've got to offer. Present company excepted, of course. Drink anyone?"

He offered the bottle, forgetting it was empty, and then searched in vain among the bottles on the table—gin, bacardi, Martini, vodka, rum—for some whisky. Eventually he hauled himself to his feet and went out. Fred watched admiringly. He doubted whether he could have stood up to win money.

"Are you drunk, pudding?"

"I may have mixed one drink too many."

She was sitting upright in the armchair, with her feet tucked up beneath her bottom. He found it difficult to focus on her.

"What was this bet you had with Oliver?" she said.

The question sobered him a little.

"How did you know about it?"

"He told me tonight. He said he won me in a game of poker. I was asking why he hadn't paid me the hundred pounds for entering the contest."

"What did he say?"

"He said 'Ask Fred.' Then he said if nobody else round here was honouring gambling debts, he didn't see why he should."

"Nice of him."

"What's it all about?"

Fred tried to sit up, but his head began to swim. "Long story," he said.

"Well, tell me. I think I've a right to know."

He got a hold on himself. "We played poker here in July. Me, Trader, Oliver, a couple of others I can't remember. There was a big hand at the end of the evening and it was really between Oliver and me. He put five hundred pounds down, and I didn't have enough money. So he said that what I could offer was a night out with you. I said okay because I thought I'd won anyway. I didn't give it a second thought."

"But he won?"

"Yes, and afterwards he said it was a night with you, not a night out, if you get the difference."

"I'm a big girl now."

"Anyway, I told him to forget it and said I'd pay him the five hundred. Which I will. So you forget it as well."

After a while, Camilla asked: "How are you going to get five hundred pounds?"

Fred stirred himself in his chair; he was falling asleep.

"Oliver's in no hurry."

"I wouldn't say that."

The man in question returned, clutching a bottle of Macgregor's whisky and a packet of playing cards. He put them both on the small table, sat down and started to open the bottle.

"Spiffing idea," he said. "Strip poker."

Camilla giggled. He poured them all a drink.

"Are you going to sleep, Fred?" Oliver asked. "If you're counting women jumping over fences, save a blonde for me."

He got up and put a Rolling Stones record on.

"Who's game for a game then?" he asked.

"Okay," said Camilla. "Wake up, Fred."

He opened his eyes and stared at the new whisky on the table in front of him. Mick Jagger was shouting quietly a long way away.

"Got any cigars, Oliver? It's difficult to fall asleep with a cigar in your mouth." The cigar's aroma, pleasant but pungent, was sufficient to keep sleep at bay.

"We're playing strip poker," said Oliver Oswald, shuffling the pack. "I'll give you five cards each, okay?"

"I don't want to play strip poker," said Fred.

"Don't be a spoilsport," said Camilla.

He had drunk too much to tell how drunk she was. He took a sip of the whisky. It seemed to go straight to his head without bothering about his stomach, and he put the glass down.

There were five cards in front of him, including two aces.

"Fred's all right," said Oliver Oswald. "What have you got, Camilla? A pair of tens? I've got damn-all."

He stood up and removed his jacket, revealing a

pair of royal blue braces over his white shirt. His shape precluded the use of a belt.

"What fun," said Camilla, pouring more whisky.

Small men with tiny hammers had begun work at the front of Fred's head. He gazed at Camilla, still sitting upright in her chair, smiling happily like a child at a party. Reality seemed to be moving away from where he was. More cards appeared. Fred took off a sandal. Oliver took off his tie. Camilla lost both her shoes. A warm silence had replaced Mick Jagger.

"When I was eighteen I tried to visit a nudist camp," said Oliver Oswald. "But I didn't know the difference between naturist and naturalist. I wound up having a miserable weekend in Wales studying chalk flora and butterflies."

"Give them a good shuffle," said Camilla. "I've only got three items of clothing left. You men wear too much."

"Where's the loo?" said Fred.

He wondered, when he reached it, why he was playing strip poker and he glimpsed the answer briefly through the alcoholic clouds. They were in Oliver Oswald's house, drinking Oliver Oswald's whisky, and Oliver Oswald wanted to play. Guests forfeited certain rights.

He lurched along a corridor wondering what to expect when he got back, but the game had waited for him and nothing had changed except that Tim Hardin was now singing.

"Come on, Fred," said Oliver Oswald, dealing cards. He studied his and the others and then took off his shirt.

"Christ, you're fat," said Fred.

Camilla hummed "Lady Came From Baltimore" with Tim Hardin and poured herself another drink.

"Cards! Cards!" she said.

Oliver dealt her the worst hand of the evening and said: "Sorry, dear."

She stood up to undo some buttons at the back of

her dress which fell to the floor. Her breasts bulged from a small white bra that didn't go over her shoulders, but only under her arms. Her matching pants were brief. She stepped out of the dress and draped it over the back of her chair. Oliver watched, as if in a stupor, then pulled himself up quickly and dealt more cards. He was taking off his trousers before Fred had seen what cards had been dealt.

He sat back in a pair of bright red underpants, his paunch protruding from the top like a pregnant woman's. This is where the photographers of the local newspaper should be tonight, Fred thought. Councillor Oswald entertains the carnival queen. Consenting adults in private. Consenting privates in adults.

He tried a little more whisky to dull the growing pain in his head. Five more cards appeared and as he was still wearing jeans and a shirt he leaned forward to look at them, feeling it was his turn to lose. But he had three eights, Oliver had a pair of kings, and it was Camilla whose hand added up to nothing. She undid her bra and dropped it on the floor with the casualness of someone removing their gloves. Tim Hardin sang "Baby Close Its Eyes".

"Your breasts are quite beautiful," said Oliver Oswald in awe.

Camilla looked down at them. "Aren't they?" she said. She ran her hands over them seductively. Fred realised with a shock that she was enjoying showing herself, that she couldn't wait to get her pants off. He realised with an even bigger shock that it was exciting him. One of his several problems had just disappeared. He moved, for comfort, in his chair.

"It doesn't look as if Fred is going to lose this," said Oliver Oswald. "It's between us."

"Why don't you call it a tie?" said Fred. "She's shown you her breasts."

"Deal the cards," said Camilla.

She received two sevens and two nines. Oliver had three eights.

"You lose," she said. "I have two pairs."

"Three of a kind beats two pairs, I'm afraid," said Oliver Oswald. As if embarrassed by the requirements of the situation, he got up and went over to the records. He put on Bob Dylan, increased the volume and rearranged the records in the stack. His white fat legs looked like tree trunks.

Fred watched Camilla. She slid her pants off with her back to him. Her bottom was almost as sun-tanned as the rest of her. Oliver Oswald came back and looked at Camilla as if he had not seen a naked girl before. His penis jumped in his pants like a snake in a sack.

"Well, that's it," said Camilla, standing between them. "I lost."

"Thank God you did," said Oliver. "You're gorgeous."

She turned round gracefully, a fashion model with no clothes, and then laughed. "Perhaps I should work in a strip-club and get paid for it."

"Let me know if you do. I'll get a season ticket."

"Shall we dance? I love Dylan."

As he stepped forward gratefully, to accept her invitation, she deftly pulled his pants down.

"I don't think it's fair that I should be the only one naked in here," she said. "Golly, I **do** turn you on."

"I've never denied it, dear. But you don't seem to turn Fred on. He's asleep."

The drinks had finally caught up with Fred and he was slumped in his chair now, chin on chest. A half-full glass of whisky was on the table in front of him, surrounded by the cards of the last hand, and a scarcely smoked cigar balanced precariously on the rim of a china ashtray. Fred dreamed of a fat naked man dancing with a small, blonde girl who was naked, too. Their feet barely moved but their bodies swayed to the distant music until the formal structure of their dancing melted into something more intimate: their hands explored each other's bodies, giving and receiving pleasure. The man's hands covered the ground slowly, thoroughly, and settled eventually on the girl's buttocks so that her feet were able to leave the ground and meet behind the man's back.

They moved, but no longer to the music.

Seven

"Don't you want to join us?" I was recently asked by an acquaintance when he ran across me alone after midnight in a coffeehouse that was already almost deserted. "No, I don't," I said.

Kafka

The following morning Fred took his hangover, like a limp, to Trader Ryan's shop.

He had woken with an ominous dryness in the throat and a blurred pain just above the heart. Ailments multiplied when he climbed out of bed. His kidneys, which he had ignored for twenty-five years, demanded his attention now with an insistent throbbing. He wondered fearfully how many gallons of beer they had been obliged to process, but the calculations had barely started when a new pain was born in the pit of his stomach. Appendicitis? Peritonitis? His heart pounded irrationally. His hands shook.

"I am not a well man," he said out loud. The mirror confirmed it. He was beginning to look terrible. All colour had fled now from his face and the dark, herring-roe rings beneath his eyes, intermittent visitors over the years, had assumed an unwelcome permanence. The horizontal lines across his forehead were also here for good, and several spots of mysterious origin were threatening to erupt up and down his nose. Nothing perhaps that sunlight, fresh air and good food wouldn't cure, but you didn't get much sunlight in England and good food cost money.

He stopped at the tobacconist and bought twenty very strong cigarettes: the time for caution had passed. The woman behind the counter scowled at him. At one time he had worried about why she so obviously hated him. It was months before he realised that she hated everybody.

Dermot's antique shop was at the end of the town, set back off the road so that tables and chairs and mirrors and lamp standards could be displayed on the forecourt outside.

In foot-high yellow letters over the door and window were the words TRADER RYAN.

Despite his "antique dealer" cards, Dermot sold anything. Inside the shop, set down with no particular eye to display, it was mostly furniture—tables, dressing-tables, two beds, dozens of chairs, a chest of drawers—and the walls were covered with pictures, all cheaply priced and most of them old and somehow depressing. But although this seemed to take up most of the space, there were hundreds of other articles presumably bought at random and lying now wherever there was room: a violin, a policeman's helmet, a model galleon, a sword, an umbrella, an American flag, an old typewriter, a pile of records, an oil lamp, some old books, a pair of bellows, a wooden African head, a bird cage, some candlesticks, a few old clocks, a wire fender, a set of scales, a brass beer-warmer, a set of dominoes, a toy car, two ship-to-shore telephones, a stuffed fox in a glass case, a coal scuttle, a very old radio, an antler hat-stand, a brass tray, a pair of coal tongs, a wall poster of Humphrey Bogart, a pair of riding boots, some postcards, a fruit bowl, and a blue biscuit tin with angels on. In a display case on one wall were hundreds of medals, some won in Army boxing rings but most of them rewards for more serious battles, and with them were a handful of plaques for forgotten athletic achievements. In another display case there were coins, each in their own plastic envelope and priced way above the face value of their day.

On a table in the middle of this chaos, two hamsters played in a cage, and next to it lay what looked like a chest wig.

After Fred had been there for some minutes, pondering over this bizarre collection of goods, the proprietor appeared from a staircase at the back which led up to the flat where he lived. He was wearing an old army greatcoat and looked as if he had woken up only very recently.

"What year is it?" he asked. "Morning, Frederick. I've got a mouth like a zoo-keeper's gumboot."

Fred waved one arm to embrace the whole shop. "I'm not surprised. This joint smells like a Peruvian knocking shop. Do people buy this rubbish?"

Dermot reached over for the cigarettes in Fred's hand and took one. "Of course they buy it. I'll sell you something before you leave."

"It's a living, I suppose. Buy cheap, sell dear. But what are you contributing to the greater good of mankind, Dermot?"

"Very amusing, first thing in the morning. Have you got a light?" He lit his cigarette, inhaled and coughed. "Actually, I had a social conscience once. I decided to hitch-hike to India to help with the hungry millions, but after three days in France I had to come home on account of I was bloody starving. Do you want a coffee?"

He disappeared up the stairs at the back of the

shop and shouted to his wife.

Fred went over to the pile of books. He rejected Seton Churchill's **General Gordon** and picked up a dust-covered copy of Hitler's **Mein Kampf**. On the fly-leaf was the inscription: "G. Why not see the other man's point of view! M." He opened the book and read: "Today the whole of our public life may be compared to a hot-house for the forced growth of sexual notions and incitements. A glance at the bill-of-fare provided by our cinemas, playhouses and theatres suffices to prove that this is not the right food, especially for our young people." Hitler Slams Sexual Permissiveness. Gas Chambers Not G-strings, He Tells Our Reporter.

"Mrs Ryan will be serving coffee," said Dermot. "Consider yourself privileged."

Fred put the book down. "Where do you get all this stuff, anyway?" he asked. The different methods that people devised for surviving in this world never failed to impress him. In twenty-five years he had not had a single idea.

Dermot sat on the table and looked at the hamsters. "It comes to me three ways. People come in and sell me things. I go to auctions. And then I clear out houses when the owner dies."

"How does that come about?"

"The estate agents ring up. I pay ten pounds and empty the house so that it's ready to be sold. It's a hell of a job, really. I can't pick and choose. I have to clear the whole lot, and eighty per cent is rubbish. Still, you never know what you are going to find."

Fred sat on a chair marked one pound in yellow chalk and put his feet up on another. He pointed at the coins on the wall. "Do you have many of these?"

"A ton. Do you realise that there are threepenny bits that are now worth a hundred pounds? I collect anything, really. I've got a dozen books of stamps upstairs."

"Philately will get you nowhere."

"I've heard all the philately jokes, Frederick."

"Oh. Which is the best?"

"I always say we deal in everything here from philately to cunnilingus."

"Is that what you always say, Dermot? What are the medals?"

"That one's the Hong Kong Plague Medal."

"The what?"

"The Hong Kong Plague Medal. The one next to it is the Messina Earthquake Medal. There were over seventy thousand people killed in an earthquake in 1908 and the Italian Government struck a medal."

Fred stood up as Mrs Ryan appeared with a tray bearing three coffees. At twenty-nine she looked tired and pale, but was very beautiful. Ten years ago, Fred thought, she must have been sensational. He saw so little of her that he had forgotten how attractive she was. He had even forgotten her name. Louise? Lena? Lesley? Her fair hair was done up in a bun as if her appearance didn't matter, and she was wearing a long red robe which stretched from neck to feet. The Ryans liked eccentric clothing.

"Coffee is served," she said. "Good morning, Fred."

"My wife makes excellent coffee," said Dermot, handing him a cup. "She also sings beautifully and plays the oboe."

"Dermot doesn't like women to have vertical talents," said Mrs Ryan, smiling. She pulled up a chair to the hamsters' cage and prodded the wire front. "Did you know that hamsters mate one day in three and fight two days in three? Just like human beings."

Fred watched Dermot smiling at this remark. In her company he was a different man.

"How are you, Fred, anyway?" she said, abandoning the hamsters. "It's a long time since I saw you. I understand you've become a sort of drop-out?"

"Drop-out? I never got in."

"If they put his brain in a cuckoo it would fly

backwards," said Dermot, stirring his coffee.

"Sometimes I think that they have already put your brain in a cuckoo, darling."

Dermot smiled at Fred. "I've got her just where she wants me, but don't tell anybody."

"What do you do, Fred?" asked his wife. "Just lead a life of pleasure?"

Fred grinned at the wildness of the guess. "Pleasure is a luxury that I've given up. It's as much as I can do to satisfy the necessities."

Mrs Ryan frowned. "I never discovered what exactly you were after, Fred. I mean, what do you **want**?"

Fred looked at Dermot's wife and envied him. This girl was something like it. He tried to frame a reply for her.

"I think what I really need is fame," he said slowly. "Total, screaming, overwhelming fame. Not tin-pot notoriety among a few people in your own line of business, but my face grinning from every newspaper column and television screen. I want to wear a disguise when I go shopping and still have people clamour for my autograph. I want to be woken up each morning by the thud of fan-mail on the mat. I want incessant phone calls and invitations. I want mysterious women to whisper that fame is an aphrodisiac as they grope blindly for my trousers. After all," he finished, "you have to be pretty well-adjusted not to resent obscurity, and nobody has ever accused me of being that." He laughed at his own reply and wondered if it were true.

"What you actually need is a wife, Fred," said Mrs Ryan, ignoring all this. "Marriage would clear your mind wonderfully and focus your energies."

"I haven't got any energies," said Fred. "I'm into lassitude."

"My wife is a great expert on marriage," said Dermot.

"Well, I've been married a long time," she said. "You haven't."

"Ouch," said Dermot, laughing.

His wife stood up. "I can't sit around here chatting all day, anyway. Be sure that Dermot invites you to my birthday party, Fred. I'm going to be thirty. We're having dinner on a bus."

"On a bus?"

"That's right."

She collected the coffee cups and walked across the shop.

"You're a lucky man, Dermot. A wife with brains."

He should waste his time chatting to psychiatrists when there were brisk, sensible young ladies about who could slice through the fog and show him simple truth! If he had married he **would** be different.

He stood up again and looked round the shop. He hoped to find something that he wanted so that he could give Dermot some business, but what use to him was a wire fender, a pair of riding boots or a chest wig? And the brass beer-warmer would seem a little flash in the Cellar.

Suddenly, on a table among a pile of records, he saw what looked like a water-pistol. He picked it up and aimed at the door handle. It was less than five inches long: he had had bigger pistols as a boy.

"What's this?" said Fred. "Is it a toy?"

"That ain't no toy. That there is a real Belgian pistol, a .32 Bayard. Very dangerous."

"Where the hell do you get something like that?"

"I got that one clearing out a house. It's amazing the things little old ladies have tucked away in their bedroom drawers. That one had half a dozen bullets with it."

He opened a drawer beneath the table. "Here they are." He put six bullets into Fred's hand. "You wouldn't believe it. I get offered a revolver or some sort of firearm every other week. I've got two out the back, a Mauser pocket model that looks a bit like that, and a Mannlicher from the First World War."

Fred studied the Belgian pistol. It felt snug in his hand.

"Where did you get them?"

"Ex-army officers. They bring them home from the wars and don't know what to do with them. The Mannlicher had been greased and hidden in an old army sock for fifty years. There was one of those amnesties on, when you're supposed to hand over your old firearms, no questions asked. A colonel brought it into town, intending to hand it over apparently, then he saw my place and came in to see whether I'd offer anything."

"What did you pay?"

"I gave him a fiver. I didn't want the gun, but I rather liked the old boy. And he was obviously hard up. But mostly I refuse to handle guns. You can get into a lot of trouble."

Fred continued fingering the Bayard.

"What did you pay for this?"

"Just ten pounds for clearing out the house."

"It's a lovely pistol."

Dermot nodded. "Very compact, not too heavy. You can buy it, if you like, to shoot Oliver Oswald's balls off. Then he'll stop pestering you."

"How much do you want for it?"

"A fiver?"

"Profiteer." Fred put the gun down and pulled a five-pound note from his back pocket. Then he put the gun in one trouser pocket and the bullets in another.

Dermot took the money and laughed.

"What on earth do you want it for?"

"I don't know. I could shoot tin cans off fences, couldn't I?"

"You could. Come on, it's Saturday. I'll shut the shop for a couple of hours and we'll go and have a drink."

They went out into the street.

"I told you I'd sell you something," said Dermot.

Sundays were especially evil. Unable to prepare anything as exotic as roast beef and Yorkshire pudding, and not having a fridge for fresh food, he lunched on something out of a tin, usually baked beans. He had other reasons, too, for disliking Sundays. The public houses kept absurd hours, opening late and closing early so that it wasn't worth the effort of getting there; the shops shut up, which cleared the streets of people; the television set vibrated with the sound of sad-looking people singing one hymn after another and, to cap it all, the rest of the population did not work either, which seemed to Fred to steal what little advantage he had.

He ate the beans on toast with no enthusiasm and washed his plate, and then tried to read the Sunday newspaper that had been delivered to him ever since he could remember. It seemed to contain the same big star life-story every week: Bronx-tenement-to-Hollywood-penthouse. It was surprising that there was anybody left in the Bronx tenements, or that any room remained in the Hollywood penthouses. He put the paper down and wondered whether he was in the right mood to add a few verses to "Coffins Are Comfortable". What he could see of it so far made him think that it stood a chance of sliding into one of those serious weekly papers that, as a nod to some obscure intellectual clique, published the occasional piece of verse that nobody could understand. But first he would count his money. He kept it, now that his relations with the bank had cooled, in an oval, red Embassy Corona tin by the side of the bed and when he emptied it he saw that it wouldn't take much counting. The coins, mostly brown, came to just under three pounds, and there were ninety-five pounds in notes. He was better off than he had thought, but if he paid the bills which kept arriving so regularly and now lay unopened on the desk in the corner of his bedroom, he was probably bankrupt. He went over to the desk and picked up the bills and then he put them down again without opening them: happiness did not lie that way. He turned instead to the long row of paperback novels that ran along the floor against one wall. They were arranged in alphabetical order, from Kingsley Amis to Gordon Williams. He bent to pick one up but was distracted by the dust and the carpet fluff that lay around them. One day he would buy a vacuum cleaner.

He went through to his living-room where the cheap television stood neglected in one corner. Days passed without his switching it on, but Sunday afternoons posed special problems that perhaps only television could solve. He turned it on and the sound of gunfire filled the room. The newspaper said that it was a film about the passions of a retired cavalry officer. He turned if off and switched on his transistor radio. "Welcome to the sunshine of Windsor Park, Belfast," it said.

"Not now," said Fred, and went back to his desk. He got out his red notebook. Many very short poems spattered its pages, which were mostly filled with longer poetry of his own, quotations of somebody else's that he had liked, or just straight paragraphs about nothing in particular. It was what Fred had instead of a diary. He picked up his pen and wrote: "Your grandmother's funeral/Could have been worse/Loved hymn/Hated hearse." He read it through and then tore the page out and screwed it up. Many pages had been torn from the book over the months, but Fred found it difficult to decide what special qualities were attached to those that had survived. He finally decided that an hour could usefully be killed by inventing the world's longest palindrome. He had seen an eleven-word one somewhere which he should find easy to beat. But it was more difficult than he had imagined. Did you start at the beginning or the end? Or both simultaneously? He had just decided to start in the middle and work outwards when his doorbell rang.

"Hello, pudding," said Camilla, marching past him into the flat. "I knew you'd be in, doing damn-all, just waiting for me to drop in and brighten your life."

He followed her into the living-room, where she kicked off her sandals and sprawled in one of the armchairs.

"This flat is filthy," she said. "I must come round and clean it some time."

"I don't know why you haven't already. The joint's a health risk."

It was the first time they had met since the evening at Oliver Oswald's nine days earlier. Her relentless pursuit of him built up his confidence, and his earlier misgivings about plunging in again were beginning to fade. She was wearing a red skirt that was so short that Fred found it necessary to sit on the floor beside her. He kissed her thighs.

Camilla looked at him but didn't smile.

"You've been ignoring me again, Fred. Why? I thought you loved me. Why haven't you called? We have a phone. It's not because of your—what shall I call it—loss of libido?"

He looked at her and thought: She's ready. She'll marry me.

"That which was lost is found," he said.

"Really?"

"Your shape changes mine."

Camilla greeted the news with a broad smile. "Placid but not flaccid," she said. "You are placid, you know. I always think of you as placid."

"Is that bad?"

"Probably not. But it would be quite nice if you kicked a window in once in a while, or hit somebody."

"That's where I'm going wrong." He lay back on the floor. "It's probably my diet. You are what you eat and I'm not getting enough raw steak." It was an idea he had developed over his baked beans: it was all a question of food. A man who had just eaten a large steak, helped along by a bottle of wine, was perceptibly bouncier than someone who had dealt with his hunger by eating a ham sandwich; food could change your attitudes as much as alcohol.

"Diet is nothing to do with it. It's because you're not happy."

"What?" Fred sat up, interested.

"I went to the library and looked your problem up. Happy people are energetic people. Depressed people just sit around. Your sex life is the first thing to suffer."

"But are energetic people happy people?" he asked. "Would a five-mile jog before breakfast bring a smile to my face? Or would I need to be smiling to embark on the jog?"

"The fitter you are, the happier you feel."

"And in no time at all I'd have bought a suit, found a highly paid job, got myself a dinky little sports car . . ."

"Lovely!" said Camilla, hugging her knees. "Why don't you do it? My father **would** be pleased."

He lay back on the floor again, depressed at how little she understood. "That isn't what life is about," he said.

"Oh, come on! It would be lovely. Your life is so, well . . . miserable."

"Life isn't about smart suits, fat salaries, flashy sports cars. Those are just the props that some people need to endure it."

The strength of feeling that he had put into these two sentences discouraged Camilla from further debate, and she picked up the Sunday newspaper from the floor and began to flick through its pages.

"Do you dream?" she said eventually, reading from the paper. "If you don't dream it could result in a serious disruption of a man's personality."

"I have nightmares. Does that count?"

"When you dream your eyeballs go round and

round as if you were looking at something."

He watched her reading the paper, sitting upright in the chair, her long blonde hair falling forward over her chest. If he got the suit, the job and the sports car she would probably come to him not only with enthusiasm but also with her parents' blessing, but because his life was a mess she hovered nervously on the edge of it, waiting for some semblance of order to be introduced.

Fred resented this. He disliked the idea that getting married was like applying for a job, with your qualifications and possibilities carefully scrutinised before you heard whether you were suitable.

It was a gesture of faith that he needed now from Camilla, and he would only get it by persuading her to marry him. The Trader Ryan theory, that with sufficient enthusiasm a man could marry anybody, would face a stiff test, but as Camilla had been complaining for weeks that he was ignoring her his new approach ought to be welcomed.

He lifted a leg in the air and gently kicked her newspaper.

"Let's go to bed," he said. "It's the same as a five-mile jog, only more enjoyable."

Camilla dropped her paper and stood up quickly.

"I thought you'd never ask."

He grabbed hold of her leg and pulled her towards him. "Take your knickers off—I want to kiss you."

Fred proposed to Camilla on a bus. It was a large green double-decker that had been converted into a restaurant. Guests ate upstairs, ten either side of a long, candle-lit table that stretched the length of the vehicle, and drank downstairs where the bus seats had been replaced by a small cocktail bar and several old red armchairs.

The eighteen guests invited by the Ryans to join them for Mrs. Ryan's thirtieth birthday party were mostly her friends rather than Dermot's, and Fred knew few of them. There was a man called Snellock in a Chester Barrie suit who introduced himself as a poverty lobbyist; a girl called Min, short for Araminta, who was tall and pale and who, according to local legend, had once, orifices unrecorded, satisfied four men simultaneously; a man called Duncan who had bought the bus cheaply, converted it himself, and was now busy every evening providing dinner in unusual spots, sometimes abroad; and several young married couples who lived near the Ryans.

The bus rumbled out towards the country in the early evening while Mrs Ryan's guests drank wine downstairs. Dermot introduced Camilla to his wife and Araminta to Fred.

"This is Cardboard Fred, pole-squatting champion and organ-grinder," he said.

"I wouldn't mind grinding his organ," said Araminta dreamily.

"You can't," said Camilla. "It's mine."

Dermot decided to tell the poverty lobbyist about poverty.

"When I call at houses now to buy something they keep offering me their animals," he said. "They say they can't afford to feed them any more. As pet food prices go up, animals are being put down. They don't want to sell them. They just want me to take them away."

"Do you kill them?" asked Mr Snellock.

"Certainly not. I sell them. I sold seven dogs last month. My wife wouldn't let me kill them. She has a thing about animals."

"It comes from having a birthday on August the twelfth," said Mrs Ryan. "Grouse shooting starts then. Next month it's partridge shooting, the month after it's pheasant shooting and the month after that fox-hunting starts. It's a massacre out there."

"If my wife had any money she'd open a hostel for buggered goats," said Dermot.

Duncan, the bus owner, told one of the guests that the bus did indeed have a lavatory and that it was at the front upstairs. The guest wandered off, impressed.

"That reminds me of my practical joke," said Dermot. "You know this transparent stuff they wrap cheese in? I once went round every lavatory in a hotel, lifting the seats, covering the top of the bowl with the stuff and then putting the seats down..."

Everybody was laughing.

"Of course, I wasn't there when it all happened, but I know it was bloody funny."

The bus was out in the country now, labouring up a steep hill. Their destination was a local beauty spot where the bus could stop for dinner, at the same time providing the guests with a marvellous view of the countryside.

Fred filled his and Camilla's wine glass. He was glad that Mrs Ryan had never met Oliver Oswald. His absence was one of the evening's bonus points.

A song called "Velvet Mornings" was playing over the bus stereo. A lady with dyed blonde hair and a foreign accent was talking to Mr Snellock about the fundamental concepts of life.

"Why does she dye the roots of her hair black?" Camilla whispered.

Fred kissed her. The decision to risk everything—rift, rejection, ridicule—by asking her to marry him had cheered him up enormously. It was suddenly quite clear to him that this was the first essential step in his rehabilitation. The wine gave him hope. He stood there, quietly confident, and listened to the chatter.

Mr Snellock had a plan to save the world: free travel. It would eliminate mistrust, he said, and result in a meeting of minds. We all had to get together and see each other's problems. End insularity.

"Who is going to pay for this free travel?" asked the lady with the dyed hair.

"Well, we all will in different ways," said Mr Snellock.

"So much for free travel," said the newly blonde lady.

The bus pulled into a car park high up in the hills. It was to here that families drove on Sunday afternoons for their weekly hour of fresh air. Tonight in the clear evening sunshine the English Channel could be seen shimmering on the horizon.

They all went upstairs and found seats at the long table. The pre-cooked food came up in a lift at the back of the bus: pâté, chicken véronique, blackberry mille feuilles.

Dermot, feeling obliged in the new setting to weld these disparate guests into a cohesive whole, told the table the story of his career as a professional interviewee.

"I used to apply for dozens of jobs and get at least ten interviews a week," he said. "They always pay your expenses for interviews, and mine were quite something. I was making about sixty pounds a week when that was a lot of money."

"What happened if they offered you the job?" asked Camilla.

"There was never any danger of that," said Mrs Ryan.

"Works all right for people who can't think of anything better to do with their time," said Dermot. "Hey, I can't talk about myself all evening. Somebody else talk about me."

"You look terribly smart tonight, Trader," somebody told him, "and well-scrubbed."

Fred realised with surprise that Dermot was wearing a suit. The white shirt was tie-less and open-necked, but it was definitely covered by a suit.

"He makes a special effort for my birthday," said Mrs Ryan.

"I have a bath every August," said Dermot, "even if I don't need one."

"I think you should propose a toast to Lena," said Mr. Snellock. "It is her birthday."

"Gladly," said Dermot. "I invite you to drink to

my wife. A truly remarkable lady. What she has to put up with doesn't bear thinking about. And here she still is, healthy, happy and lovely."

Everybody raised their glasses of wine. Mrs Ryan kissed Dermot's cheek.

Fred watched with growing astonishment. This wasn't how he had imagined the Ryans' marriage at all. His picture had been of a fun-loving, irresponsible husband, determined at whatever cost to get a laugh out of life, and of a suffering, neglected wife, alone more often than not, at home. But that wasn't how it was. They were perfect partners and deeply happy, despite Dermot's little jokes. It was there now for all to see.

Somebody started to sing "Happy birthday to you" and everyone joined in.

Fred lit a cigarette from a candle on the table and held Camilla's hand.

"They make a good couple, don't they?" she said.

"Just what I was thinking."

"Do you think that marriage is going to make a comeback?"

"I didn't know it had been away."

She brushed away a speck of ash on the table cloth and said: "You're so conventional, Fred."

"I must be getting old. Nobody has ever called me that before."

She smiled at him, not quite in the way that he would have liked.

"Well, of course, you're not in many ways, but you cling to the traditional values, like marriage, family units, all that stuff."

He saw that if this was indeed his image it was in his interests at least as far as Camilla was concerned, to lose it. "Actually," he said, "I don't believe in anything. It's called nihilism."

"I do. I believe in pleasure."

"That's called hedonism," said Fred. "How do you become a member?"

"You don't join it. You do it."

Down the table the party had broken up into many conversations. Mr Snellock was defending communism to Duncan, while Dermot was working out his lifetime's consumption of beer and cigarettes.

"I've been in pubs nearly every day since I was twenty and I never drink less than six pints a day. On top of that I smoke about thirty cigarettes a day." He was writing on a cigarette packet.

"Is he trying to tell us something?" asked Min.

"So in the last sixteen years I have drunk thirty-five thousand pints of beer."

"Amazing you're sober," said his wife.

"And smoked a hundred and seventy-five thousand cigarettes."

"Shut up and put your lungs back in."

"No, really," said Dermot, shaking his head. "It's frightening, isn't it? The average smoker gets through twenty miles of cigarettes in a lifetime."

Fred drew heavily on his own and refilled his glass. A new optimism took care of the health fears that Dermot was inviting.

He put his hand over Camilla's and said: "I'll tell you one thing I believe."

"Do."

"I believe that you should come and live with me. Immediately."

She stared at him, wide-eyed, and began to smile.

"What a beautiful idea! Why didn't you think of it before?" The smile vanished as suddenly as it had arrived. "What are we going to live on?"

"If you move in I shall find a job. Promise. Whether you work is up to you."

Camilla nodded. "That's **much** better than a proposal of marriage."

"Regard it as the modern equivalent among we unconventional folk."

"Daddy will say, 'Are his intentions honourable?' Actually, he probably **will** say that!"

"Reassure him. Better still, don't tell him."

"I'll have to." She finished her wine and turned to

kiss him. "What fun it will be! Look, I can't cook very well. Do you mind?"

"I'm quite used to bad cooking."

He was surprised that she was so keen on the idea. Women were unpredictable creatures. Only three months earlier she had preferred an abortion to marrying him but now the idea of living with him touched a responsive nerve and filled her with glee.

The eating seemed to be over and people were moving slowly down to the bottom deck to drink at the bar. Fred and Camilla were the last to leave.

Downstairs Dermot was buying the drinks.

"A very happy evening," Fred told him.

"Much better than one of your hairy switched-on groove-ups. What are you drinking?"

"I'm going to buy some champagne. If they have any on this here vehicle." He went to the bar and pulled out two five-pound notes.

Mr Snellock was now defending the broad strategy of the South African government. It occurred to Fred that the man was incapable of seeing the bad in anything; if somebody mentioned Belsen, he would probably chat happily about the benefits of the medical research that went on there.

Duncan produced a bottle of champagne and some glasses. Fred filled four and gave one to Dermot, his wife and Camilla.

"Why the devil don't you two live together?" said Mrs Ryan. "It's none of my business, of course. I just enjoy organising other people's lives for them."

"That's what we've just decided to do," said Camilla.

"Wonderful," said Mrs Ryan.

"Perhaps you'll get married," said Dermot. "I'll dance at your wedding."

"Camilla isn't a supporter of marriage," said Fred. "Apparently it's out at the moment."

"Not with us, it's not," said Mrs Ryan. Her arm was round Dermot's neck. "It would be the making of you, Fred."

Fred had a deep fear that too much talk of marriage was going to frighten Camilla off. He felt like a man who had hooked a wonderful fish but was going to need patience and skill to bring it to the river bank. He held her hand very tightly.

"But that's not true," Mr Snellock was saying, flushed now with the wine. "There are no dictatorships west of the Elbe."

Fred, feeling bullish, leaned across to him. "Belt up and have some champagne," he said.

Eight

Birth, and copulation, and death
That's all the facts when you come to brass tacks
Birth, and copulation, and death.
T.S. Eliot "Sweeney Agonistes"

It had been a long, hot summer. Between February and August only five inches of rain fell, instead of the usual twenty-eight, and farmers panicked as wheat and barley yields slumped. Some had to use winter feed supplies on their cattle. Others fed them with silver birch leaves.

Partly because of the heat and partly to please Camilla, Fred spent a lot of his time at the swimming-pool where he swam length after length while waiting hopefully for some dramatic indication that fit bodies did indeed house happy minds.

He also waited for Camilla. Deciding after drinking Lena Ryan's birthday wine to tell her father that she was going to live with Fred was one thing; doing it sober seemed more difficult. The Boyd family had now been back in England for five months and Camilla had still not found a job. The airline that she had written to had asked her to apply again in six months. Her father's disapproval filled the house. It was not the time to tell him that she was off to live with Fred. Instead she looked for work. She met none of the obstacles that always faced Fred: the world was full of people who were anxious to pay her to sit in their office. The younger the boss, the higher the pay and—it was implied—the easier the work. After several interviews, each involving higher salaries than the last, Fred had visions of Camilla keeping him in some luxury. Eventually she accepted a secretarial job with a smooth property developer because, she said, his office "smelt of money". Her salary was more than Fred had ever earned, a piece of information that he thought prudent to keep to himself. It was also more than enough to impress her father who, after a lifetime in the forces, knew very little about wage inflation.

It seemed a good moment to tell him that she was going to leave home.

"What do you want to do that for?" he asked.

"I'm going to live with Fred," she told him.

"What do you mean?" he replied. "Live with him?"

"Fred has a flat in the town. I'm going to live in it."

The Air Commodore, who until this moment had been more occupied with the anagrams of **The Times** crossword than with the conversation with his daughter, laid the paper in his lap and said: "Oh no you're not. We don't want any of that."

"Any of what?"

"Any of this pre-marital stuff. You're only nineteen, for God's sake."

"Oh, daddy," said Camilla, laughing. "Half the girls have got two kids by the time they're my age."

"And no husband," said her father. "Was this Fred's idea?"

"He wants to marry me."

"I could tell that."

"But he has no job."

"So you're going to keep him?"

"Golly," said Camilla. "Welcome to the twentieth century."

Her father ignored this. "I absolutely forbid it. Use your brains. Show some patience. A commitment like that now could ruin your life."

When Camilla told Fred about this conversation later she played down the strength of her father's opposition to the idea of their living together, and merely conveyed a vague impression of fatherly disapproval. Fred concluded that this was an initial reaction which, with the right behaviour on all sides, would be softened, even reversed. It would probably take more than a box of cigars for the Air Commodore, or a bottle of Port, but if he found himself a job and dropped in on the Boyds occasionally, charm at full strength, there was no reason why he should not win them over.

But having decided that these should be his tactics, he was immediately thwarted. If he suggested that they spent the evening at Camilla's, she discovered a new film that they should see. If he told her that he would pick her up at her home, she insisted that they met in town. The message was unspoken, but Fred received it clearly enough: Camilla was keeping the men in her life apart.

He lived with this for a while, feeling that events were slipping away from him but not knowing how he could prevent the slide. Lurching between extremes of emotion, he entered new fields of depression, compiling wills and visualising the guests at his own funeral.

Camilla became restless, too. The idea of living with a man—with Fred—had promised to open up her life, and her delight had been genuine. Having it extinguished so quickly had unsettled her. She was gloomy with Fred and fractious at home so that her parents were kept aware of her displeasure. She took to going for long walks alone in the country, which unnerved her mother who saw rapists behind the hedgerows.

And then, to everyone's surprise, the problem vanished—at the wedding of Ant and Wendy.

On a sunny September afternoon they sat in the back row of a beautiful old church in the country and watched Wendy become Mrs Brock. She stood upright and self-assured in her long white dress while Ant, an inch or two shorter, fidgeted nervously. Fred watched, fascinated. The £20,000 house with its multi-chime doorbell would soon be hers. Cupid or cupidity?

The tiny church was full of men in rarely worn suits and ladies in strange hats. One seemed to be wearing a red bowler. The vicar, a short, plump man with a high-pitched voice, shouted his lines with a vehemence that was almost menacing.

"Firstly, it was ordained for the increase of mankind according to the will of God, and that children might be brought up in the fear and nurture of the Lord, and to the praise of His holy name."

It was a long time since Fred had been in a church and the irrelevance of what the vicar was saying shocked him. No wonder people wore funny hats in church.

"Secondly, it was ordained in order that the natural instincts and affections, implanted by God, should be hallowed and directed aright; that those who are called of God to this holy estate, should continue therein in pureness of living."

Fred looked at Camilla to exchange an expression on all this—an expression that would have involved pulling down his eyebrows so low that both eyes would have completely vanished; but she was staring at the scene entranced, like a child at its first film.

"Thirdly," shouted the vicar, "it was ordained for the mutual society, help and comfort, that the one ought to have of the other, both in prosperity and adversity."

"I now pronounce you bubble and squeak," Fred whispered, but Camilla waved him to silence. When the couple had been married she joined the rest of the congregation in reciting Psalm 67. It was quite a paradox, Fred thought, as he mumbled football results against the general drone. He had been the advocate of marriage and Camilla had been its critic.

"Let the people praise thee, O God: let all the people praise thee."

"Tottenham Hotspur, nil, Aldershot, seven," said Fred. "More news at half time."

Outside in the sunshine they posed for photographs. Wendy had a little smile, correct and controlled. Ant, even paler than usual, looked like a man who had just lost both testicles in a crooked card game. Fred mentioned this fact to him between photographs, but Ant said he had an appalling hangover from the previous evening.

"I'm not like you, Fred," he said. "I'm not used to alcohol. Thanks for the present, by the way. Whatever it was."

"It was a bedside lamp."

"Come here, Antony," said the bride. "A photograph with my mother."

"Be fruitful and multiply," said Fred.

"Not bloody likely," said Ant.

Later, when the perspiring guests had been guided cattle-like into a nearby hall and glasses of champagne had been thrust into every hand, there was an outbreak of the sort of polite conversation that takes place when you don't know who is overhearing you. Opinions were ventured but never riskily: the bride was beautiful, the bridegroom was brilliant, the bride's mother was an absolute angel.

Camilla sat silently through it all, her mind on other things, and then suddenly she gripped Fred's arm and said: "Let's do it."

"Do what?" he answered. Knowing her lovely spontaneous nature, he imagined that she wanted to make love.

"Get married."
"Really?"
"Yes, really."
"Certainly. Yes. When?"
"As soon as possible."

Fred took her hand and kissed it. It seemed unfair to him that such a stunning girl should attend someone else's wedding. A bride, on her big day, should not have to face such competition.

"What brought this on?" he said.

"Oh, it was beautiful in there." She meant in the church. "It's the first wedding I've been to for years and I'd forgotten how lovely they are. So moving."

It certainly churned my tripes up, thought Fred, but he said nothing. The shallowness of her reasoning wasn't important to him. He had wanted to marry her for months.

"Anyway, it's the only answer. My father will never allow me to live with you if we're not married. I know it isn't fashionable, but I don't want to hurt him. He's been bloody good to me."

"What do you think he would say if you told him we were getting married?"

"He likes you. He thinks you're clever. He said there's more to you than meets the eye. It's just that you haven't got a job."

"I'll get one."
"I love you."
"So do I."
"I know, but do you love me?"
"Very droll."

Bride and groom reappeared in different clothes. They were flying to Rimini that evening. The bride wore a green two-piece suit, and carried a large dark green handbag.

"What do you suppose she's got in there?" Fred asked, interested. "Sleeping pills? Tear-proof mascara? Freshen-up tissues? Anti-chip nail lacquer? Smudge-proof eye-shadow? By the time she's lugged that lot to the Adriatic she won't be any use to Ant."

"You're a cynical bastard," said Camilla. "Sometimes you frighten me."

"Sometimes I frighten myself, darling. Kiss me and make me mortal."

Suddenly—briefly—he was a new man. The future was no longer a weight on his shoulders: it was in front of him, bright, clear and inviting. First, a job—any job for a start. Then marriage to Camilla. The missing ingredient was about to be added to his life.

For the first time for years he had energy to spare. He jumped out of bed within minutes of waking. He cleaned the flat. He dusted obscure corners that spiders had made their own, hoovered all the carpets with a huge cleaner that he borrowed from the pet shop downstairs, bought a sponge mop and washed every stain from the vinyl-tile kitchen floor. The mouse will be pleased, he thought. He cleaned the sink, the bath, the oven. He washed the windows. He mended a loose tap, bought two new lampshades and fixed up a holder for the kitchen roll. Then, still bubbling, he redecorated the bedroom in deeply sexual purple. When he had done all this, and stood back to admire it, he found fresh work and fresh energy. He made a bookcase out of new house bricks and planks of pinewood, and a table lamp from a large green gin bottle. He arranged to hire a colour television because that is what Camilla had at home and, for the same reason, he inquired about the cost of having a telephone installed in the flat. Next, as if the restorative work should not be confined to the home, he made an appointment to see a dentist about replacing a filling which had left him months ago in the company of a lump of toffee. Finally, after four days in which he had hardly smoked and didn't drink at all, he bought himself a new sports coat and went out to get a job.

It was the day that the local newspaper appeared and he headed straight for their offices to buy a copy.

Half the paper was advertisements, many of them for jobs.

The receptionist was a young girl made up in a fashion that was inexplicably catching on: the edges of her eyes were covered with what looked like black boot polish, and she had a white, cruel mouth. Fred gave her a big smile.

He was so keen to find a job that he opened the paper immediately without bothering to leave the office. The front page carried a photograph of Ant's wedding—the two stars and all available relatives—but Fred hurried past that. When he reached the Situations Vacant page his heart sank momentarily at the familiar list of unfamiliar jobs. There was work for a deburrer and training would be given to a suitable applicant, and there was good news, too, for any out-of-work agricultural bulk-blower drivers.

Fred's eye ran down the page in search of the remotely possible.

"There's got to be a job somewhere," he told the girl.

"There's one here if you want it," she replied.

"What is it?" Fred asked, but before she could answer he was carried away by a picture of himself with notebook and six finely sharpened pencils, a Press ticket in his hat-band and a green eye-shade (if reporters wore a green eye-shade). Scoop Carton Flies In To Trouble Spot.

"Selling space," said the girl. "Have you got any O-levels?"

"One or two."

"If you're interested I'll call Mr Davies."

Fred nodded slowly, and wondered how you sold space.

The girl strolled sexily through a door at the back of the office and reappeared a few moments later with a very tall, cadaverous man of about fifty.

"Mr—?" he said.

"Carton."

"Step into my office, Mr Carton," he said, and led Fred back through the door.

It was a small, untidy office with three telephones, a typewriter and several hundred old newspapers piled up on any flat spaces that were available, including the floor.

"Take a seat, Mr Carton. How old are you?"

"Twenty-five," said Fred, sitting down in front of Mr Davies' crowded desk. Mr Davies tried to find sufficient room to commit this information to a large sheet of headed notepaper.

"Tremendous. Ideal," he said. "I'm the advertisement manager. What I need is an assistant. His job is (a) to chase up advertising copy on the phone, (b) to visit shops and firms to try to persuade them to advertise in the paper. A good salary plus commission. I need someone who is (a) personable (b) persuasive (c) keen."

Fred sat back and listened to Mr Davies talking about the job. He was vaguely thrown by the alphabetical nature of his conversation, but he smiled enthusiastically. It soon dawned on him that after a lifetime of selling Mr Davies knew no other method of human discourse. He was trying to sell the job to Fred and telling him that with eleven O-levels he was just what they were looking for. He was a master of ingratiation, somewhat superfluously, Fred thought, as he wanted the job anyway. From an adjacent room came the chattering of reporters' typewriters, and somewhere in the offices a telephone was always ringing.

"When could you start?" asked Mr Davies.

"When you like," said Fred. "I'm between jobs at the moment." He thought it wise not to reveal exactly how long his intervals between work lasted: a new image of an industrious and ambitious young man was being constructed quickly.

"Let's say Monday week," said Mr Davies, writing on his sheet of notepaper. "Give me your address."

Winthin half an hour Fred was back in the street, not in the least surprised at the ease with which he had found himself a tolerable, well-paid job. It was exactly what he had expected to happen once Camilla had given him a reason to act. He walked briskly into the town, amused at a new jauntiness he detected in his stride, and decided that after all his domestic labours and particularly with this final triumph he could reward himself with a drink.

Trader Ryan sat alone at the bar of the Cellar. He was wearing a new suede, waist-length jacket and jeans.

"Where in hell have you been?" he said. "Four days' absence. I hope you've got a note from your mother."

"I've been busy," he said, "starting my life. A pint of bitter, please, Miranda, and give Mr Ryan what he wants." He sat on the stool next to Dermot and smiled at him. "I'm getting married," he said.

Dermot dived off his stool in a mock faint and lay motionless on the floor.

"It's a bigger shock than you think," he said eventually when he got up. "My wife bet me a tenner that you marry Camilla. Why am I always wrong? I've only got to say 'good evening' and the bloody sun comes up."

"You've been chosen as best man."

"I'd be rather good at that. When is it all happening?"

"Soon. We're fixing it up tonight." He picked up his drink. "Cheers."

"Cheers, and congratulations. Won't you have to get a job?"

"Got one."

Dermot put down his drink and laid a hand over his heart. "It's too much. I can't take it. Where's the job?"

"On the newspaper."

"On the newspaper? You don't know a dangling participle from a dangling testicle."

"The advertising side."

"Ah."

"Congratulations, Fred," said Miranda. "I'll buy you a drink myself."

Fred emptied his glass instantly. It was time, he decided, for a little roistering.

"There are a few things to arrange," he said.

"First, an engagement party."

"What sort of wedding receptions does the hotel do upstairs, Miranda?"

"Good but pricey," she said, giving him a drink.

"The Air Commodore will pay. I hope."

Dermot rubbed his hands together. "A lot of new opportunities for getting stoned out of my box are beginning to emerge," he said. "I like it."

"Even if you lose ten pounds to your wife?"

"Behind every silver lining there's a cloud, kiddo. Listen, is all this serious?"

"I start work a week on Monday. It's time you advertised your shop in the paper. A nice little three-column job with your picture in the corner . . ."

"Blimey, he's working already. How about some champagne?" He pulled a role of ten-pound notes from his pocket. "Bring us a bottle of something good, Miranda. This is history."

Fred now had a feeling of well-being that was wholly alien to him. He took the champagne happily. The future had fallen quite firmly into place and nothing could dislodge it. Even the prospect of work failed to depress him. When the lunch-time drinkers arrived for an hour's escape from their offices he felt that he was one of them. Dermot watched him.

"Don't get too jubilant," he said. "Marriage does have its drawbacks."

"Yours looks pretty good to me."

"Not always. Lena had a right go at me this morning. A real shouting match, venom dripping from her fangs. 'I'm not your toy! I'm your wife! I'm a person!' 'Shut up, or I'll put you back in the cupboard,' I said. You've got to handle them."

"Every divorce begins with a marriage," said Miranda. "Take Oliver Oswald."

"Where is he lately, anyway?"

"He hasn't been in," said Miranda.

"Good," said Fred.

"He's probably arranging his divorce," said Dermot. "I bet Trixie comes out of it rich. That's marriage, you see, Fred. When it goes sour your wife pisses off with half the house you're trying to buy."

"I'm not trying to buy a house," said Fred. He was drinking in earnest now—holding his glass, not leaving it on the bar. Nearby, a group of solicitors, all in dark grey suits, were having gin for lunch.

"He's always impeccably dressed," said one.

"Absolutely immaculate!"

"He and I used to carve up the county court together," said one of them in a rich voice.

It is into this privileged landscape that I am about to insinuate myself, thought Fred. He wouldn't have the abundant cash of the lawyers, but he would be better off than most people in the country, or the world. Without imposing any strains on himself he would be able to live well (bank account with cheque card, holidays with sun, dinner with wine). He would be absorbed unnoticed into the middle-class mosaic.

The champagne bottle was empty.

"During the First World War," Dermot told Miranda, "it was illegal to buy someone a drink in a bar. Would you tell Fred that this law has now been repealed?"

"Lager, not champagne," said Fred. "We married men have to watch the pennies."

"Where is the future Mrs Carton, anyway? Why isn't she here, winding large gins down her throat like a proper wife?"

"She works. She earns money. But tonight she is dining at my flat and all the arrangements are going to be made. Dates will be fixed, invitation lists made out. You'll be kept awake by the sound of happy laughter."

He left the Cellar an hour later, high on hope and alcohol, and bought some food for dinner: fillet steaks, eggs, mushrooms, camembert, celery, and a bottle of wine.

The lager and the champagne raised the prospect

of another stupefied afternoon and he went to lie on the bed. He slept immediately. Soon he was getting married in a cathedral. Sun streamed through painted windows high above the crowded congregation. Fred and Camilla stood expectantly before a bishop, but something was wrong: Camilla was completely naked.

"It was ordained for the increase of mankind according to the will of God," said the bishop, distracted by Camilla's body. Behind, somebody leaned forward to stroke her bottom. Fred turned to push the hand away, but when he faced the front again the bishop was fondling her breasts.

"Let's get out of here," said Fred. "They're all going mad."

"We can't go yet," said Camilla. "We're not married yet."

The crowd pressed in on them to see more of Camilla. The air was heavy with sex.

"Leave her alone and get on with it," Fred told the bishop. He withdrew his hand, embarrassed, and tried to pick up the threads of the service. It became horrifically clear to them all that beneath the flowing robes of his cassock he was masturbating like a demented monkey.

"Natural instincts and affections implanted by God," he mumbled, "hallowed and directed aright."

The congregation was jostling them from all sides now and Fred began to feel like the object of a political riot with no police around to shield him from the mob. Camilla fell over under the pushing, and the bishop dropped his prayer book and fell gratefully on top of her.

"My dear, my dear," he whispered, but Fred woke up without discovering what he had in mind.

He lay on the bed for a while searching in vain for some meaning to the dream, and then he got up and had a bath. His head was clear: alcohol's after-effects had been defeated again. He washed his hair, found himself a clean shirt and went into the kitchen to prepare the food. He got out his chip pan which he hadn't used for months, filled it with vegetable oil and cut up some potatoes. He put pepper and a knob of butter on the steaks, cut up two tomatoes and washed the mushrooms.

There didn't seem to be a lot more that he could do so he laid the table, put out the cheese and celery, and then sat in an armchair and waited for Camilla.

A train of thought which began with the cheese on the table took him back to the Unit. If his life was about to become the happy, well-organised existence that lives were supposed to be, he would presumably be marked down as one of the Unit's belated successes, unlike Joe. Joe died after eating a large lump of cheddar cheese on top of some anti-depressant pills, but even before choosing such a novel way to go he had established himself as one of the more unusual patients in the building.

A highly regarded form of treatment had been the psycho-drama in which a patient was invited to act out a crucial scene in his life, with other patients playing supporting roles. They rehearsed it on their own and then played it out before the patients and the staff, who were supposed to discuss it afterwards in the hope that this would help the patient.

Joe's psycho-drama involved donkeys. He had served as a sergeant in India during the war and had been responsible for a dozen pack mules. One day the war had moved on. The pack mules were no longer required. Joe had to shoot them.

Fred's role in the psycho-drama was an officer drinking in a bar. Joe came in looking depressed.

"You look depressed," said Fred.

"I've just shot my donkeys," said Joe, and began to cry.

Joe's being upset over dead donkeys bemused the doctors, who had every reason for believing that mental problems emanated from one's family. Joe didn't have any family. He only had donkeys.

"Did you regard the donkeys as your family?" one of the doctors asked.

Joe nodded tearfully. The doctor looked relieved. The following night Joe ate half a pound of cheese.

Reliving this strange episode, Fred forgot the time. Camilla had promised to arrive at seven o'clock. It was now almost eight. He shot out of his seat in a panic. She had never been late before.

He checked the change in his pocket for a phone call and went into the hall. A strong intuition that something was disastrously wrong came up to him. Don't over-react, he told himself. Everybody is late at one time or another. He left the flat and went down the steps to the street, quiet now in the evening sunshine.

As he opened the door of the telephone kiosk he saw the short, shapely outline of Camilla in the distance, blonde hair, blue shirt, blue jeans, walking slowly towards him. He didn't hurry to meet her; he needed time for his relief to subside. She waved from a distance, and turned her face up to be kissed when they were together, but there was a look in her eyes that he hadn't seen before. She was frightened.

"I was just going to ring you," he said. "I thought I was going to have to eat all this food on my own."

He took her hand and they climbed up the steps to the flat.

"I'm sorry I'm late," she said. "I had to go to the doctor."

"Why? What's up?"

She shook her head. "Nothing." She waited while he unlocked the door. "I had to collect a prescription for my mother."

"Come and have a look at my handiwork," he said, shutting the door. "I've been very busy. I've even got a job."

"You haven't?" She seemed more surprised than pleased.

"It sounds perfect," she said when he had told her about his interview at the newspaper office. "When do you start?"

"Monday week. Come and see my paintwork in the bedroom."

They walked slowly round the flat as Fred showed her the changes that had taken place that week: the painted bedroom, the new bookcase, the lampshade, the sink that now shone.

"I have also eliminated dust from my life," he said. "You will notice the newly clean carpets, the sparkling hall, the kitchen floor that your shoes no longer stick to."

"It's lovely, Fred," she said sadly.

He was disappointed at her reaction to his exertions but he didn't dare to pursue it. She had bad news written all over her now.

He didn't want bad news.

"Are you hungry yet?" he asked, when she had sat down. She nodded unconvincingly.

"I'll open the wine."

He found an elaborate bottle opener, the souvenir of a distant holiday, and looked at the label on the wine bottle. It said Nebiolo Spumante. You'd better be good, he thought. He took two full glasses to the living-room, gave one to Camilla, and sat in an armchair opposite her. What he wanted to do was roll across the floor and slide her jeans down but the atmosphere made it painfully inappropriate. He searched his mind for some light conversation, and finding none there searched his pockets for a cigarette.

"Let me have one," Camilla said, leaning towards him. "This is nice wine."

"A cigarette?" Fred said. "You don't smoke."

"Well, I do now. What sort are they?"

She held out her hand but Fred was reluctant to give her one. How many thousands of pounds would your first cigarette eventually cost you? To introduce someone to smoking should be illegal.

"Come on, Fred," she said.

He saw her expression and gave her the packet. She lit one and puffed inexpertly. She coughed and laughed.

"What's so soothing about these, then?" she asked.

He pushed an ashtray across the floor towards her. "You've got to work at it, kid. It takes years of practice."

Camilla held the cigarette between finger and thumb, putting it in the middle of her mouth and sucking and blowing.

"What else did you do today?" she asked. "Apart from get a job."

"I celebrated with Trader at lunchtime. He brought champagne. This afternoon, I can't think why, I fell asleep." He remembered his dream and told her about it. He brought in every detail, prolonging the story, as if non-stop babbling could keep out the bad news that was beating at his door.

"I don't think I'd like to get married naked," she said.

Fred watched her trying to remove some ash from her cigarette. "Where would you like to get married?" he asked. "We've got some arrangements to make—remember? Church? Register office? Mosque? Pagoda?"

Camilla gave the ash removal all her concentration.

"My parents wouldn't be too wild about a register office wedding," she said finally.

"Have you told them yet?"

"Not yet."

"Why not?" An answer was slow in coming and Fred said: "Do you want me to talk to your father? I'll go round and ask for your hand, if you like. I know it sounds a bit macabre..."

Camilla was now holding her cigarette in her lap and staring down at it.

"There is a complication," she said. "I don't know how to tell you."

Fred, as alert now as she was subdued, said: "With words, beautiful. We always use words round here. An invaluable aid to human communication."

"Okay, I'll use words." She took another nervous drag on her cigarette. "I did go to the doctor's surgery tonight. That was why I was late. But it wasn't to get a prescription for my mother. It was to hear the result of a test. I'm pregnant. Again."

Fred could barely control his relief. Was this all? It wasn't even bad news, he realised quickly, because if Air Commodore Boyd was going to provide any opposition to their wedding he would change his mind pretty smartly when he discovered that his daughter was expecting a child. Events for once were putting the right cards into his hand. He went over and sat on the floor beside her.

"That's not so bad, is it?" he said. "I wondered what awful secret you arrived here with. You looked like death."

"You don't think it's so bad?"

"I wanted a child last time, if you remember."

"I remember."

"But, blimey, you're fertile, aren't you?"

"They've only got to hold my hand and I'm a week late."

"Let's have some more wine."

He fetched the bottle from the kitchen and refilled their glasses.

"I must start cooking in a minute," he said, resuming his position on the floor.

"I'm not really hungry yet, Fred."

"It's the cigarette. You'll have to cut out that foul habit while you're pregnant."

"I didn't enjoy it, anyway."

She drank some wine and looked sad.

"Well, no abortions this time. I swore I'd never

have another and I never will."

"Abortion? I should hope not. It's prams and baby-cots this time, Miss Boyd. It looks as if I got a job just in time."

He smiled up at her but the green eyes were filled with misery.

"Come on, beautiful, smile. It's going to be all right. In fact, it's going to be marvellous." He got on one knee to kiss her and she smiled briefly. He wondered if she was going to cry.

He sat down on the floor again and a thought occurred to him.

"I suppose there is one question that might spring to a person's mind," he said.

"What's that?"

"Don't take it as a criticism or anything. I'm actually glad that you're pregnant. But some people would think that the first thing you would have done after the trip to London last time was get round to a family-planning clinic."

"That was the first thing I did."

"What happened?"

"They wouldn't let me have the pill. They said it wouldn't suit me. So they gave me an IUD but it made me bleed. In the end I was fitted for a diaphragm. You know that."

"So I do. So where was the diaphragm?"

"Where it usually is. In my bag. You don't wear it all day, you know. You put it in when you need it. I didn't know that I was going to need it."

Fred was mystified. Camilla began to cry.

"I have to tell you the truth," she said, sobbing. "It's not—"

He couldn't hear her for the sobs.

"Sorry. I didn't hear."

"It's not yours."

She cried quietly. Fred sat, unable to speak, the colour draining from his face. He knew now what the expression "his blood ran cold" meant: he was shivering. He held the floor firmly and didn't look at

Camilla. It was a long time before she spoke again.

"You know whose it is?"

Fred thought, didn't trust himself to speak, and shook his head very slowly. The room seemed suddenly to lack oxygen.

"It's Oliver's. You know that. You were there. It's all your fault . . ."

She was crying again. Fred didn't move. As usual, the virus of happiness had produced the antibody of disaster, but this time he was surprised: in even his lowest moments he had never considered this possibility.

Camilla, on a different tack now, had control of her tears. She wiped her eyes with a Kleenex and put it in her handbag on the floor. She wanted to talk.

"It was the night of the carnival. We went to his place for drinks. I didn't know I'd need the bung. We were all drunk anyway. Then that stupid strip poker. It was all because ofyour crazy bet with him. I don't know . . . I thought I was saving you five hundred pounds. It seemed such a little thing . . ."

She bowed her head. Fred didn't move, didn't speak.

"We were dancing, if you remember. He got excited and sort of slipped it in. It was a joke. We were laughing. I wasn't even sure that it was in. He said, 'That clears Fred's debt.' Then he gave me the hundred pounds that he'd bet me. It sounds odd now, but it seemed so harmless . . ."

Fred sat on the floor and stared into the future. He saw nothing. He wanted to light a cigarette but he knew that his hands would shake. The evening sun pointed incongruously into the room.

Camilla watched him for a long time.

"Say something, Fred. Say something, for God's sake."

He looked for words but a numbness had gripped his brain. He tried to shake it off, tried to find something to say about what she had told him, but it was going to be some time before he could talk about it.

They sat beside the laid table, Fred on the floor, Camilla in the chair, wrapped in their own thoughts and each wondering what the other was thinking. Presently questions began to form in Fred's mind: Did Oliver Oswald know? If not, would she tell him? If so, would she marry him?

But he had received all the news that he could take today and he didn't want his questions answered.

"Fred," said Camilla, "are you all right?"

He felt very tired now as if all strength had left him. He nodded slowly; it seemed an immense effort.

She sat waiting, not knowing what else she could say. Ten or fifteen minutes slipped by before she finally gave in.

She stood up.

"I'd better go," she said. She looked at Fred, who didn't move, and then stooped to collect her handbag from the floor. For two or three more minutes she stood and watched him and then, quickly, she left the room.

A few seconds later Fred heard the front door close behind her, but it was another two hours before he got up and went slowly to the kitchen, where he dropped the uncooked fillet steaks into his orange plastic pedal bin.

Nine

Tomorrow has been cancelled due to lack of interest.
Graffito in Hampstead

Fred went to Dover to say good-bye to his mother. He caught a morning train to London, and another out of it from Victoria. The green fields of Kent had turned brown in the heat. The heat filled the train. Fred pulled down a window but the air that rushed in seemed, despite its motion, to be as hot as the air already in the carriage.

His father had worked in the office of an insurance firm, a fact which so dismayed Fred that he had never felt like asking precisely what he did. When he had died three years ago, from a heart attack at fifty-six, Fred's mother had sold their house and moved swiftly back to Dover, where she had spent a happy childhood. With the several insurance policies that her husband had taken out, she now lived in comparative affluence in a new, grey-brick bungalow not far from St Margaret's Bay.

She was a short, cheerful woman who made

friends easily with her contemporaries, but was permanently puzzled by her only child whom she called "too thoughtful". Life had always seemed simple to her. Within minutes of his arrival she had him installed on her new sofa, a cup of tea on his knee. She talked.

"You've picked a beauty of an afternoon to drop in. I'm playing bridge at four o'clock. But it's lovely to see you. It must be months since you came down. What are you doing now? You're not the world's most prolific letter-writer. People ask me what you're doing and I have to say I don't know. I feel such a fool. Would you like some biscuits?"

Fred shook his head and sipped at the tea; it was too hot to drink. The family cat that he had bought as a kitten ten years earlier stared up at him from a new fake fur rug in the middle of the room.

He said: "Who do you play bridge with?"

"Oh, friends. I'm meeting people again that I went to school with. It's lovely. Of course, they never left Dover. We have a lot to talk about. And they keep saying 'When is your son coming down?'"

Fred found himself a cigarette. "Well, here I am. I thought I'd drop in to make sure that you are all right. I think you're marvellous, mother. You've created a whole new life for yourself."

"And I love it," she said, nodding. "But what about you, Fred? What are you doing?"

"Well, nothing. I'm between jobs at the moment."

"Oh, Fred." There was slightly more disappointment than disapproval in her voice. "Sometimes I think that I should have stayed up there and kept an eye on you."

Fred smiled at her. "You're all right. That's the main thing."

Her hair was only partially grey, and her round face was unlined; she seemed to be getting younger.

"Yes, I'm fine but what about you? Do you want any money?"

Fred shook his head quickly. "I wouldn't mind an ashtray," he suggested.

She went out to the kitchen to find one. Fred looked round the room. All the furniture was new, he realised, as if his mother had slowly shed every vestige of the past and was determined to start afresh. He leaned forward and tickled the cat.

"Hallo TFC," he said. He had called it TFC ever since it was a kitten, but only he knew that it stood for "the fucking cat". Elderly aunts had often secretly delighted him by calling "TFC!" as they dangled a morsel before it.

His mother returned with an ashtray.

"I've seen you looking better," she said. "Are you eating enough?"

"Mother, don't worry about me. You've done your share of that."

"You were never any trouble, Fred. I just can't understand why you haven't found the right job. Your father could have got you into insurance, but you refused to have anything to do with it. I always hoped, with the exams you got, that you would become a teacher. There's no money in it, I know, but it's so . . . worthwhile."

Fred had forgotten these earlier ambitions of his parents. It seemed a long time ago. The old feeling of guilt at the disappointment he was causing returned briefly, but it had lost its bite.

It was all irrelevant now, and his only concern was to see that his mother was contented in her new life on the coast. They talked for an hour and he kept the conversation away from himself.

When he left the bungalow a weight had been lifted from his mind.

Black clouds drifted across the sky as he reached home. They were an unfamiliar sight after the hard, dry summer and people were looking up at them in the street.

Fred left the station and walked quickly into town. The temperature had dropped and the farmers' prayers had been answered: the drought was almost over.

It was early evening now, and the workers were queueing for buses home. What did they have to look forward to? An evening in front of the television, no doubt. The average Briton now spent eight years of his life slumped in front of the box. It frightened Fred to think about it.

He decided that a couple of drinks would help him on his way and headed for the Cellar. For a change, Miranda was presiding over an empty bar. He gave her a big smile and took a stool at the counter.

"You look unusually cheerful," she said. "Getting a job obviously suits you."

"The martyrs sang as they went to their deaths, Miranda. Give me a large whisky with ice, please, and a smile."

He felt strangely light-headed as if, without sufficient ballast, he could soon be floating round the room. He held the edge of the counter firmly.

"Poor old Fred," Miranda said as she placed the whisky in front of him. "What are you going to be when you grow up?"

There was something comforting about her efficiency—she could carry the load for two. Perhaps a tall brunette was what he needed after the unhappy months with a short blonde.

"Miranda," he said, "I have a proposition for you. A proposal, even. How would it be if we got married?"

"Pretty bloody awful, I should imagine. What brings this on?"

"Should I take that as a rejection?" His whisky glass was empty already. "Miranda, baby, in an ideal world—"

"In an ideal world you'd be ideal. But you're not. So we won't. Would you like another drink?"

"I'm not like the average person, admittedly. I'm a particular sort of person."

She took his glass and refilled it.

"Bum, I believe, is the generic term."

He shook his head. "Okay, I'll call it off. I'll cancel the invitations. It's a small world that blows nobody any good nor iron bars a cage."

The double whisky on an empty stomach had affected him more than several pints of beer.

"I'll have one of your best cigars," he said. Expense no longer mattered.

Miranda went to the end of the bar where over-priced cigars were displayed in a small show-case. Fred picked up the evening newspaper that had been left by an earlier customer. In Ireland, devout Christians were enthusiastically removing people's kneecaps with Black and Decker drills; in India, fifty thousand people had died in a cyclone; in Dresden, in East Germany, the flower of British youth had rioted after a soccer match and made Churchill's activities in the same city look like benevolent reconstruction.

He put the paper down and thought: I wish that I could have been somebody else, just for a few minutes, to find out whether being a human being felt like this for the others, too.

Miranda brought a selection of cigars. "Take your pick. I don't know—whisky, cigars, no job. It beats me how you survive."

He took the cigar that was nearest and spent some time getting it alight.

"It beats me how I survive as well," he said. He sucked at his cigar. His survival had mostly been on a day-to-day basis, and when he looked back at it now he was surprised at how much survival he had assembled. There had been many times, when the pressure was there, that he had marvelled at the way that he and everyone else had managed to get by. He would meet somebody after a week and have to restrain himself from congratulating them. There they were—they had done it somehow, found twenty-one meals, seven nights' sleep, avoided any of a hundred possible disasters and appeared again—upright, solvent and well. But nobody else, apparently, regarded it as an achievement. It always surprised him.

He watched the cool Miranda slicing lemons at the back of the bar. Survival posed no problems for her. She would go from this job to another and from there into marriage without so much as a change of expression. No doubts would assail her, no opinions would be revised. Life, from where Miranda was sitting, appeared to be ridiculously easy. The subversive idea that it could be slightly less fun than an impacted wisdom tooth had obviously never occurred to her businesslike brain.

He tried to picture what marriage with her would be like. She would be all bustle and efficiency, meals on time, bills promptly paid, but his lethargy, which would start as a private joke that brought them together, would quite quickly drive them apart. Would she pull him up or would he drag her down? Perhaps he would begin to share her uncomplicated view of the world: contentment could be catching. At least, with her feet on the ground and his in the clouds, the sex would be interesting.

If you must know, doctor, my personality is a fatal compound of whimsy and despair. I can't help seeing the joke through the tears in my eyes.

He looked round the bar and hoped that a friend would come in. He had a powerful need to talk. But the room remained empty and there was nobody he could count on seeing.

"Has Trader been in?" he asked Miranda. Even now, with no customers, she had found something else to do: she was breaking up the ice from the ice machine and dropping it into a green plastic container on the bar.

"He was in early. Said he had to go home to supper."

"Beans on toast."

"He said seafood."

"Sardines on toast. I'll have another whisky."

He had nearly drunk enough now: one more drink and he would be ready.

Two men came in, shaking rain from their

jackets. The deluge had started. They went to the bar and ordered brandy. The mood was appropriately sepulchral.

Fred, on the way with the drink now, beckoned Miranda. There was nobody else to explain to.

"You see," he said, "you have to play the game of life with the cards that you've been dealt."

As usual, Miranda had the answer.

"Nobody knows what cards they **have** been dealt, though. That's the whole point."

Fred considered this. "I'm beginning to get an idea, and from what I can see it's a rough old hand." He finished his drink and stood up. "I have seen the future and it doesn't work."

He walked out into the rain. Within a few yards it had drenched his shirt, but he walked on at the same unhurried pace. He wondered, as he walked, where he had gone wrong. It didn't matter, but it gave him something to think about.

Should he have used his time differently? Had his interests been too limited? Why hadn't he become absorbed with potholing or pottery, acting or painting, football or sailing, music or motor-cars, or any of the other minor obsessions which evidently carried millions of people from one day to the next?

It seemed a stupid idea and he dismissed it. It was all very well wondering where he had gone wrong, but the sinister truth was that he was not convinced that he had. At his most neurotically apprehensive, he even had a crazy suspicion of happiness. To achieve it would somehow be challenging the gods. He knew intuitively that if the day had ever arrived when he had all the things he wanted—whatever they were—he would step off a pavement with the sun in his eyes and vanish under a sixty-seater coach.

He walked on through the rain. His walk was more urgent now; occasionally it seemed to be more of a march. He passed the petrol station where he had once worked, and the old people's home, a transit camp between useless living and useful dying. A lonely lorry rumbled past. It was mid-evening and the town was surprisingly deserted: a nation was communing with its television. Dusk was falling and the rain, if anything, was heavier now.

The town hall clock broke the silence as he reached his flat. The chimes seemed to bring him back to life, and after that he started to do everything slowly but carefully as if there was no room for a mistake.

He climbed the steps to his door and let himself in. He put the hall light on, and went straight through to his own bedroom, where he went immediately, almost anxiously, to a chest of drawers. He rummaged through one of them until he found the Bayard automatic. He looked at it for a few moments and then placed it on the green duvet on his bed. When he had done this, he pulled a towel off the back of a chair and went over to the mirror to dry his face and hair. He combed his hair with his fingers, dried his hands, returned the towel to the chair and then went back to the chest of drawers. This time he found the six bullets that he had bought with the gun, and a half-empty packet of cigarettes. He went back to the bed and tried to get all six bullets into the magazine, but it was built to hold only five. He returned the sixth bullet to the drawer and left the loaded automatic on the bed. Then he took out a cigarette and lit it, before sitting down at the desk in the corner of his room.

He pulled back his chair a little, so that he could open the desk's drawer, the contents of which he began to examine in detail. At the top there were only bills: water, electricity, rent, gas—even the newsagent wanted eight pounds. He pulled them out of the drawer and with them, in the same handful, came an out-of-focus colour photograph of Camilla sitting on a beach, a penny toll ticket to Clifton Suspension Bridge, a membership card to a long-defunct jazz club, a postcard from the other side of the world showing a dhow being loaded with mangrove poles, and a street map of Paris. Behind them in the same drawer were three diaries that had never been used, a pair of pyjamas that he had never worn, two books that he had never read (**Psychopathia Sexualis** by Krafft-Ebing, and **The Glass Bead Game** by Hermann Hesse), a Christmas card from an old girlfriend, a newspaper cutting and his red notebook. Drawing more frequently than usual on his cigarette, he took the last three items out and shut the desk.

He looked, first, at the Christmas card. The picture on the front was from Raphael's Madonna and Child, and written inside, in thick-nibbed fountain pen, was the message: "Every happiness, Fred—at least all you'll allow yourself to have." He stared at the card as vacantly as he had done everything else in the room and it was some minutes before he put it down. Before he did, he tore it into eight pieces, as if he found its purpose offensive, or, more probably, had sensed some accusation in its inscription. He pulled another cigarette from the packet and lit it from the one that he was just finishing, and then he picked up the newspaper cutting which he looked at, first casually and then with increased interest. It was an old story from a London newspaper which began: "One in ten of all the deaths of men and women between the ages of twenty-five and thirty-four in Kensington and Chelsea are by suicide." Fred read the article, which he had saved himself, as if he had not seen it before. "Suicides tend to increase in the middle class and decrease with poverty, say doctors. Unemployment and overcrowding have no correlation with suicide." For some time, Fred seemed undecided what do to with this, but finally he tore it up and put it with the remains of the Christmas card.

He cleared his desk of everything except his ashtray and his red notebook, which now lay closed in front of him.

It was to this book that he had returned many

times over the months, scribbling poems or questions or jokes without plan or direction, as if the wildly multiplying words could somehow stand as his witness. There had also once been the fanciful notion that he could make money from his poetry.

Eventually, he opened the book, which was over an inch thick and more than half full, but he flicked through the early pages as if he already knew them too well. It was only when he came to the last half dozen pages that he began to read every word.

I'll Be The One Standing Here

When you get back from Juan-les-Pins
And the romance is all over, my dear
When your world has collapsed and you need a kind word
I'll be the one standing here.

When he leaves you for dead in a warm hotel bed
And you know that you've wasted a year
When you drag yourself home with an ache in your heart
I'll be the one standing here.

When you return in a daze and your life is a maze
And the long future fills you with fear
When you're too sad to cry and you're too sick to die
I'll be the one standing here.

(And what I shall say is: It serves you right for sodding off with that pouf in the first place.)

She was a card, that girl.
In her heart
She wanted diamonds
But she slept with a spade
And now she's in the club.

When they came for the Jews I was not a Jew, so I did not protest. When they came for the Catholics I was not a Catholic, so I did not protest. When they came for the trade unionists I was not a trade unionist, so I did not protest. When they came for me there was nobody left to protest.

Pastor Niemöller

I think my sexual problems are reaching proportions unknown to medical science. It is no longer only pretty girls who distract me in the street. Anything between twelve and fifty slows my stride. I contemplate goalie's dives across the pavement, my tongue wedged in knicker elastic, police sirens wailing.

F.J. Carton

I am learning to bring into my voice that polite acerbity that makes people feel that far from being welcome they are not even tolerated and are under continual and scathing analysis at every moment.

Francis Scott Key Fitzgerald
"The Crack Up"

Man hands on misery to man.
It deepens like a coastal shelf.
Get out as early as you can,
And don't have any kids yourself.

Philip Larkin
"This Be The Verse"

The Eight Points for Attention are as follows:
(1) Speak politely.
(2) Pay fairly for what you buy.
(3) Return everything you borrow.
(4) Pay for anything you damage.

(5) Do not hit or swear at people.
(6) Do not damage crops.
(7) Do not take liberties with women.
(8) Do not ill-treat captives.

Mao Tse-Tung

I am sure that since I have had the full use of my reason, nobody has ever heard me laugh.

The Earl of Chesterfield

Beer makes you think.
Food makes you fatk.

F.J.C.

DEAR SIR

There is a flaw in the game of football. There are too many goalless matches. The goal posts should be further apart.

Yours etc., **Moving Finger**

There is a flaw in the game of cricket. Nineteen out of twenty-five Test matches between England and Australia were drawn. Introduce a fourth stump.

Yours etc., **Moving Finger**

There is a flaw in my personality. Wherever I look, I see flaws. I'm hypercritical. Nothing satisfies. I'm picky to a fault. Take the anthology of cliches and misprints that you call your newspaper...

Yours etc., **Moving Finger**

A POEM

The world looks at me and asks
Why is he clowning?

It should really ask
Is he waving or drowning?

ANOTHER POEM

How does a plant drink?
How does a fish blink?
How does a cyclops wink?
How does a woman think?

Coffins Are Comfortable

This morning I saw a postman
with a smoking bomb in his hand
and a letter-box full of hostages.
It would be nice if more people
had flocked to my banner, he said,
but you can never tell a blind man
what colour red is
or describe an orgasm to a eunuch.

In the under-developed territory of his mind
he chased an elusive idea.
Callouses and parcels, palaces and castles.
The epicurean delights of the postal regime
eliminate subcutaneous fat
from my bank account, he said.
Me poor, you rich.

This morning I saw a bishop
exploring a garbage can.
I'm in holy ordures, he said hungrily,
as a worm trotted up his gaiters.
Man cannot live by God alone.

This morning I saw a policeman
mugging a man in a bank
while laughing soldiers machine-gunned
selfish shoppers in the street.
I'm taking your wallet into custody,

said the policeman, jovially.
The people kept us poor,
said the soldiers.
Bang! Bang! Bang! Bang!
They lived badly. Let's see
if they can die well.

This morning I saw a

When Fred had finished reading, he opened the notebook at a new page and found a ball-point pen in his drawer. He sat for a long time, not moving, but shivering occasionally from the wet shirt on his back. After thirty minutes he wrote: "Dear World (my anonymous persecutor), This was suicide while the balance of **your** mind was disturbed," but he tore the page out immediately and screwed it up. He then sat for over an hour, staring at the new empty page in front of him. Words were racing through his head, but his hand didn't move.

I had hoped that something pleasant would happen to me before they put me away in a box, but I can see now that this was uncharacteristically optimistic.

If despair is the unforgivable sin, what does "sin" mean?

Dear Oliver, May your eager penis vanish overnight, may your testicles turn to iridium and crash through the floorboards, may your pile-infested anus implode.

He didn't know what he wanted to say or whom he wanted to say it to. He lit each cigarette from the butt of the previous one. The ash-tray on his desk overflowed.

Dear Camilla, he wrote. I can't work out whether we were unfortunate or stupid. The irony of what has happened now, just when I thought that our difficulties had been resolved, has, I fear, overwhelmed me.

Feeling that this would place too heavy a burden

upon her, he added: I exaggerate somewhat. It is only one of my problems.

He put the pen down and stared at the wall in front of him. A few minutes later when he looked back at the notebook he realised with horror that he could barely read his own handwriting. He tore the sheet quickly from the book and dropped it on the floor. He was like a professional writer now who sits alone in a tiny room and stares, sick in the heart, at the vast, empty page, wondering where all the words are going to come from.

He took another cigarette from his packet and saw that he only had one left. The discovery prodded him into action suddenly, as if he was now governed by a time limit.

He picked up the pen and wrote quickly but carefully, so that his handwriting would not betray him. He wrote:

> Dear Mother, I've made this decision calmly enough so please don't let it distress you. As you may know by now, I have recently been receiving treatment in one of those splendid social rehabilitation units that are springing up all over the country. The treatment was for depression and inadequacy and for certain self-destructive tendencies which the medical profession felt—accurately, one now gathers—they could detect in me. But the only certain method of ending depression and removing misgivings about the future lies on my bed with five bullets in it. I came home from the Unit in July feeling, for some insane reason, that everything was going to be all right, but it wasn't and it isn't going to be. Quite apart from the love affair in my life which has ended disastrously, my inability to acquire money happily is reason enough to quit. I suppose that people will say I am sick, but people never understand why others do not enjoy what they enjoy. I can tell you what I lack in one word:

enthusiasm. For anything, really. And I have no curiosity about the future. Love, Fred.

He sat smoking his cigarette for several more minutes before he added a line to the letter:

PS. I want to be cremated.

Then he tore the page from his notebook and read it and reread it for fifteen or twenty minutes. At the end of that time he put it in an envelope which he sealed and addressed.

He was in a hurry to be away now: his last cigarette was finished. He left the letter, address uppermost, on his writing-desk and went over to the bed, where he picked up the Bayard automatic. He held it under the light and examined it for several minutes, then he slipped it cautiously into his pocket and put out the light.

It was past midnight, and when he went out into the street the town was deserted but the rain had stopped. The clouds had moved on and the sky was a ceiling of stars.

Fred paused for a while, as if wondering which way to go, and then, with his hand on the gun in his pocket, walked quickly towards the wide Georgian street that led up to the manor house and the park. He found as he walked that there were tears on his cheeks and, leaving them there, that they stung.

His quick stride and the cold air seemed to get his mind working again and he began to think about what he was going to do.

He regretted the stigma that was attached to suicide, the assumption of sickness. Whatever the shrinks said he didn't see why it had to be the weak or the ill who failed to love this world. A thousand people committed suicide every day. It was quite normal.

Death was a fact of life.

He reached the entrance to the park. Below, to his right, the town slept. In the moonlight he could see the dark windows in the great hall of the house. A light wind rattled the trees to produce a fresh downfall of rain.

He walked for two or three hundred yards before he came to the place that he wanted, a group of trees and bushes sheltered together in the remotest corner of the park. He looked round again. Everything was silent here except the wind.

He examined himself, absently, for signs of nerves, but there was only one word running through his mind: enough.

The bushes and trees had made a small room of this space, and he walked the length of it and back before fixing on a spot. He stood there motionless for a few seconds before sitting down exactly where he stood; the wet grass soaked his jeans immediately but he gave no sign of discomfort. He pulled his right hand from the pocket where it had been since he left the flat.

For some minutes he studied the silhouette of the gun against the sky and then, as if he had done it many times before, he put the barrel into his mouth. He aimed it upwards, pushing it against the roof of his mouth and then, with no tangible thought in his head, he pulled the trigger.

Ten

The thought of suicide is a great consolation: with the help of it one has got through many a bad night.
Nietzsche

The silence of Sunday hung over the town like a shroud. Above it, black clouds rolled across the sun promising further rain, while a fresh wind danced through the streets bearing the first leaves of autumn.

People were coping with Sunday in their different ways. Half of the male population were tampering obsessively with their cars as if the machines could not endure five days' normal use without major weekend surgery. Many of the rest slept on in bed. Some ignored the clouds and drove to the sea. A tight-lipped minority went to church.

Church bells rang across the town, shattering the silence, summoning the faithful, and in many homes people left their beds and shut their windows against the noise. Later the peace would be threatened again by the drone of lawn mowers and the caterwauling of the transistor radio.

Fred woke late. To stall all thoughts of the previous night he got out of bed directly he woke and walked rockily to the bathroom. He turned the bath's hot tap on and the gas heater on the wall burst into life. His bones still felt damp from the soaking of the night before and he made the water as hot as he could stand and then lay in it for a long time. Afterwards, he found some new, dry clothes: an old pair of corduroy jeans and a black, short-sleeve shirt. He shaved with his electric razor, combed his hair and then examined himself in the mirror. He decided, to his surprise, that he had often felt worse.

It was too late for breakfast, and he left the flat and sauntered through the deserted streets.

Like all the other shops, Trader Ryan's was closed. He had to ring the bell three times before Dermot appeared. He was wearing a garish dressing-gown in red and gold. His legs and feet were bare.

"Frederick, my boy," he said. "Come in."

"Were you in bed?"

"Bed? No. I was wrestling with the intellectual Sunday papers. Got to find out what I'm thinking. Coffee?"

"Why not?"

He disappeared up the stairs at the back of the shop and returned a few minutes later with two coffees.

"Where are the hamsters?" Fred asked.

"Sold 'em to a kid. Cigarette?"

"Thanks. I haven't got any." He took one and lit it. "How was your seafood supper?"

"Oysters, actually. I'm trying aphrodisiacs, or alleged aphrodisiacs. I'm having trouble with my organ—the swell pedal isn't working. The news is that oysters are magic. I woke up with an erection like a pylon."

Fred drew heavily on his cigarette and coughed. "You're telling me more than I want to know, Trader," he said.

Dermot laughed and sat down on a small wooden bookcase that he had been trying to sell for more than a year.

"What **do** you want to know, kiddo? You've come to the fount of all knowledge. Actually, I had something to tell you but I've forgotten what it is."

"I want to know what you make of this life. What do you **make** of it?"

"It's all going too bloody quickly. That's what I make of it. Have you noticed?"

"I can't say I have. It seems to me to be dragging unbearably."

He pulled up a chair to the table where his coffee was and sat down.

"That's because you're young, Fred. There are shocks in store for you. I wake up in the morning two seconds after getting into bed. The day goes so quickly I can't believe my own watch. It's Friday when I think it's Tuesday, it's September when I'm thinking it's still July. I'm thirty-six and I feel like twenty-five. This cradle to the grave trip is like the bloody Cresta run. It's frightening."

"Probably because you enjoy yourself."

"And so should you. At the third pip it will be too late."

"I try but it's awfully difficult."

Dermot shifted his wooden bookcase so that he was facing Fred. He looked at him strangely. "Let's have this out," he said. "I'm glad you brought it up. There are several things I want to say to you and today is a very good day to say them." He put a foot up on a chair. "Do you know why you fail? Because your attitude is too fucking timid. Not just negative, but timid. Try? You don't begin to try. You've got to go out and do the adventurous things, the things that'll enlarge your life, not shrink it. Life won't come to you, Fred. It's quite happy to ignore you. You must go to it. You're like a wallflower at a dance sometimes."

"A wallflower at the dance of life? You get a bit bloody lyrical on coffee, don't you?"

"I know it all, kiddo. And I've got your number. It wouldn't surprise me if you didn't wind up in one of those modern psychiatric joints one day, discussing neuroses with the shrinks. Well, they can't help you. Your best bet is Trader Ryan. I was fairly gnarled up myself when I was a teenager, but not for long. Being happy in this world involves no more effort than getting off your arse. Pain's easy, Fred. Do you remember saying that most people never expose themselves to the risk of anything interesting happening to them? I was very pleased when you said that. I thought, he knows at last. But the trouble with you is that you say one thing and do another. What you said was the heart of the matter. Seek out the life-enhancing things or you'll wind up in a small room never going anywhere."

"Have you finished?"

"Nearly, kiddo. Nearly. You asked for this and I'm going to tell you." He pointed his finger at Fred. "You've got to go out and make things happen in your life or you might as well lie down and die now. I wouldn't go to work in that office and I wouldn't marry Camilla, either. That's taking tablets for headaches. What you've got to do is stop what's causing the headaches in the first place. Open your life up. Wander round Europe getting jobs where you can. Just sitting down and drinking a beer in a place like Narbonne will make you feel twice as good as you ever do here. Travel down the French canals. Become a barman in Biarritz or a deck-hand in Palma. Meet new people. Change your life so completely that after a while you'll be changed as well. What you're suffering from is galloping atrophy. More coffee?"

Fred nodded. Dermot disappeared with their

cups. Fred stood up and wandered round the shop, picking up things, looking at prices.

He felt oddly hopeful, as if he had suddenly been granted some unexpected insight.

Dermot returned with two coffees and some more cigarettes.

"What I'm really here for is I'm a dissatisfied customer," said Fred. He put the automatic on the table and picked up his coffee.

"What's the matter with it?"

"It doesn't work."

"Well, I should hope not," said Dermot, picking it up. "It's a lovely little gun but those bullets would never work now. You haven't tried to shoot with it, have you?"

"I used it in the park."

"I thought you wanted it for a laugh, to produce in the Cellar, or something."

"You knew it wouldn't work?"

"I knew the bullets wouldn't. There's nothing wrong with the gun. My God, you didn't think I'd sell you live bullets, did you? You'd probably blow Oliver's head off or something."

"Or something."

Dermot drank his coffee and looked at Fred closely. Fred thought: He knows.

"Do you want your money back, then?"

"It crossed my mind."

Dermot pulled a roll of money from his hip pocket and handed Fred a five-pound note.

"You're too old to play with guns, anyway. Fancy a drink?"

"If it's not too unadventurous."

"And after that you're coming round for Sunday lunch. I've just fixed it with Lena."

"Thank her."

He drank his coffee and handed Dermot the empty cup.

"Why did you think I shouldn't marry Camilla, anyway? I thought you rather liked her."

"Actually, I thought she was rather vacuous. But as you obviously know, she's marrying Oliver Oswald. That's what I had to tell you. They were in the Cellar yesterday lunchtime discussing it."

"I was in Dover," said Fred.

"She's pregnant, apparently."

"So I believe."

"But we're not going to let it depress us, are we, or I'll split your nose open."

"Me?" said Fred. "Depressed?"

"I'm going to put some clothes on. If you go on ahead and show Miranda that five-pound note she'll turn it into gin and tonic. She's clever like that. Then I'm going to get inside your head and point you in a few interesting directions. You've reached a little crisis in your life—don't think I don't notice—but there's a new chapter coming up and I'm going to write it."

Fred walked out into the sunshine and shut the shop door.

He had intended to telephone Doctor Jago next and ask to be re-admitted to the Unit, but something that Dermot had said changed his mind. There was a more positive, more energetic, approach to life that he had not even tried. It was a philosophy that came strangely to him, but it was hugely encouraged by an extraordinary feeling of relief that he was still alive after the trauma of the previous evening.

He remembered the painter who had jumped off the parapet of the eighty-sixth floor of the Empire State Building and had been blown back by high winds on to the eighty-third. He didn't jump again. He climbed through a window. He had changed his mind between floors.

What on earth was the point of committing suicide when life was so short anyway?

He paused outside the health food shop and looked at the packets of nicotine-free cigarettes. Perhaps he would buy some of those and become healthier. A notice in the window said: If health food shops sell health food, what do the others sell? It was a thought. Cod liver oil capsules, nicotine-free cigarettes, health food—at this rate he would soon be running two miles before breakfast.

He marched down the street and found himself whistling. I'll be all right, he thought. I'll be all right eventually. Things can't get any worse. They must therefore get better. It was quite encouraging if you looked at it like that. He reached the door of the Cellar. There's nothing wrong with me anyway, he thought, remembering his joke, nothing wrong with me that a miracle couldn't put right. He smiled to himself and eased the Cellar's door open.

THE SECRET LEMONADE DRINKER
by Guy Bellamy

"A major new comic talent... I laughed and I laughed, reading it in the state of tremulous excitement which must be the nearest we novel reviewers come to an understanding of heavenly bliss... the book is a corker—witty, intelligently observed, well written and original. Thank you Mr Bellamy".

AUBERON WAUGH, EVENING STANDARD

"A very funny first novel... Bawdy, witty, sometimes touching, the book more than lives up to its zany title".

THE SUN

0 552 10796 4 75p

BOGMAIL
by Patrick McGinley

Now, why should a Priest-turned-Publican, Roarty, cook a poisonous mushroom omelette for his barman and then beat him over the head with volume 25 of Encyclopaedia Britannica?

And what is Potter, a passing Englishman, doing with the local Canon's housekeeper?

And who is the elusive, witty, mysterious 'Bogmailer'?

The answers to these and other charming Irish riddles are to be found in the pages of this wonderful novel, rich in suspense and abounding in character.

0 552 12273 9 £1.00

SUMMER AWAKENING
by Eric Malpass

A lot could happen over the long summer holidays—and in the Pentecost household it usually did. But this summer was the most eventful yet . . . With the help of an unexpected German au pair, Gaylord was discovering that some girls came a pretty close second to boats and rugger; Momma was noticing that old friend Charles was looking at her in a strange new way, and Amanda aged ten, knew she would die if Gaylord's friend Roger married anyone else but her . . . Never did the course of love run less smoothly than in the Pentecost family but before long Gaylord was wishing the summer would never end. And Momma was fearing she'd never see the end of it.

0552 10755 7 80p

BLESS ME FATHER
by Neil Boyd

Meet Father Neil Boyd, as he copes with his first confession, deals with a shotgun wedding, runs the parish bazaar, thwarts the local bookie, and does his best to outwit the Mother Superior of the Convent. Meet Father Charles Duddleswell, the plump, mischievous Irish parish priest who initiates Fr. Neil in the practical tricks of the priestly trade. Meet Mrs. Pring, the formidable housekeeper who alternately pampers and tyrannises her bachelor charges. Priest or Non-priest, churchgoer or atheist, Bless Me Father is a book for everyone who likes to have their ribs tickled and their sides split with helpless laughter.

0 552 10669 0 75p

A SELECTION OF FINE TITLES IN CORGI PRINT

☐ 10796	4	**The Secret Lemonade Drinker**	*Guy Bellamy*	75p
☐ 11163	5	**Lucia in London**	*E. F. Benson*	£1.25
☐ 11113	9	**Queen Lucia**	*E. F. Benson*	95p
☐ 10669	0	**Bless Me, Father**	*Neil Boyd*	75p
☐ 11010	8	**A Father Before Christmas**	*Neil Boyd*	85p
☐ 11149	X	**Imogen**	*Jilly Cooper*	85p
☐ 10878	2	**Prudence**	*Jilly Cooper*	85p
☐ 10576	7	**Harriet**	*Jilly Cooper*	85p
☐ 10818	9	**The Cedar Tree: A Bough Breaks**	*Michael Hardwick*	80p
☐ 10438	8	**The Cedar Tree: Autumn of an Age**	*Michael Hardwick*	75p
☐ 10755	7	**Summer Awakening**	*Eric Malpass*	80p
☐ 10756	5	**Oh, My Darling Daughter**	*Eric Malpass*	80p
☐ 10626	7	**The Long, Long Dances**	*Eric Malpass*	75p
☐ 10625	9	**Morning's at Seven**	*Eric Malpass*	70p
☐ 98081	1	**The Frank Muir Book**	*Frank Muir*	£1.95
☐ 09891	4	**Chia the Wildcat**	*Joyce Stranger*	70p
☐ 09462	5	**Lakeland Vet**	*Joyce Stranger*	70p

All these books are available at your bookshop or newsagent, or can be ordered direct from the publisher. Just tick the titles you want and fill in the form below.

CORGI BOOKS, Cash Sales Department, P.O. Box 11, Falmouth, Cornwall. Please send cheque or postal order, no currency.

U.K. Please allow 30p for the first book, 15p for the second book and 12p for each additional book ordered to a maximum charge of £1.29.

B.F.P.O. & EIRE allow 30p for the first book, 15p for the second book plus 12p per copy for the next 7 books, thereafter 6p per book.

Overseas Customers. Please allow 50p for the first book and 15p per copy for each additional book.

NAME (Block letters) . . . .

ADDRESS . . . .

. . . .